PURE
SLUSH
BOOKS

WRATH

7 Deadly Sins Vol. 5

First published as a collection January 2019

BP#00075

Pure Slush Books
32 Meredith Street
Sefton Park SA 5083
Australia

Email: edpureslush@live.com.au
Website: https://pureslush.com/
Store: https://pureslush.com/store/

Original fountain image copyright © Sarah Benton
Cover design copyright © Matt Potter

ISBN: 978-1-925536-68-3

Also available as an eBook
ISBN: 978-1-925536-69-0

A note on differences in punctuation and spelling

Pure Slush Books proudly features writers from all over the English-speaking world.
Some speak and write English as their first language, while for others, it's their
second or third or even fourth language. Naturally, across all versions of English,
there are differences in punctuation and spelling, and even in meaning. These
differences are reflected in the work *Pure Slush Books* publishes, and they account for
any differences in punctuation, spelling and meaning found within these pages.

Pure Slush Books is a member of the
Bequem Publishing collective
http://www.bequempublishing.com/

• Alex Reece ABBOTT • Sara ABEND-SIMS •
Edward AHERN • MaKayla ALLEN • Joseph
ALLISON • Shawn AVENINGO-SANDERS •
Elaine BARNARD • Paul BECKMAN • Jim BELL •
Robert BEVERIDGE • Rick BLUM • Howard
BROWN • Elizabeth BUTTIMER • Sam
CAMERON-MCKEE • Steven CARR • Guilie
CASTILLO ORIARD • Martin CHRISTMAS • Jan
CHRONISTER • Robert COOPERMAN • Mark
CRIMMINS • Tony DALY • Salvatore DiFALCO •
Judah ELI • Michael ESTABROOK • William
FALO • Gloria GARFUNKEL • Flora GAUGG •
Nod GHOSH • Geralda GJOMAKAJ • Ken GOSSE
• Roberta GOULD • Andrew GRENFELL • Shane
GUTHRIE • Jo HOCKING • Matthew HORSFALL
• Mark HUDSON • Michaeleen KELLY • Jemshed
KHAN • Ron. LAVALETTE • Larry LEFKOWITZ
• Cynthia LESLIE-BOLE • Peter LINGARD •
Patience MACKARNESS • Grahame MACLEAN •
Kate MAHONY • John MAURER • Karla Linn
MERRIFIELD • Corey MESLER • Peter MICHAL •
Marsha MITTMAN • Colleen MOYNE • Piet
NIEUWLAND • Edward O'DWYER • Emily
O'SULLIVAN • Carl 'Papa' PALMER • Ben PITTS
• Melisa QUIGLEY • Charles RAMMELKAMP •
Lisa RHODES-RYABCHICH • Ruth Sabath
ROSENTHAL • Ed RUZICKA • Jeff
SANTOSUOSSO • Gerard SARNAT • Pegi Deitz
SHEA • Cormac STAGG • Lucy TYRRELL • Alan
WALOWITZ • Michael WEBB • Jeffrey WEISMAN
• George YATCHISIN •

Contents

Poetry

Poetry

Greek Coffee

Ed Ruzicka

Have you ever wanted to strangle a friend,
no matter how much he would thrash and push?
Nick and I had been up past moon-set to whoop,
and stomp from camp fire to camp fire

at a party in New South Goat-sack Mississippi
on the ten acre grounds of a potter who threw
gigantic Raku pieces and also hosted annual
bashes under the autumnal sparks of Orion's belt.

He invited the entire Art and Classics departments
along with reprobates, half-bakes, and stray debutantes
out of the city to camp, imbibe, hoot, dance
as if there was no end to it while hills rolled

off in every direction, darkly secret and with
Mississippi's grim resolve. Disturbed
from their rounds, coyotes glared, lit irises
reflected at the edge of the woods.

Field mice nudged along their customary
paths under blown weed and thistle.
We reveled. That night some bearded satyr
grabbed my lapels and shouted into my face

"I see you at every weird party I go to"
at which I blinked, smiled. Beyond provocation
I shook my head and sauntered off. Found
a twisty little grad student's wife to get to know

in the biblical way in the cab of Nick's Silverado.
Eventually some forty of us bivouacked on slopes and knolls.
Woke to dew. My Greek friend Nick had a little blaze going.
Was rubbing his hands to warm them as kettle water boiled.

That is when it started. Nick had a metal cup,
a spoon with a ceramic design in its bowl. Nick stirred
his coffee with the spoon till it went from thin to thick,
from thick to gluck. Nick stirred and stirred. A crow

perched at the forest's edge cawing as the spoon scrapped
along cup metal. Nick hunched. The crow cawed.
There is only so much that a hung-over man
by a campfire in Mississippi can be asked to endure.

The Storm Wind

Edward Ahern

gusts and surges
like an unchained guard dog,
strewing dust and pollen,
flashing the naked underside
of leaves,
and tossing meadow grass
like ruffled bear fur,
spinning from side to side
in drunken dance,
a rioting brawl that cannot last,
and ends
with a watery flourish of thunder.

Beach Confession

Jan Chronister

Forgive me Mother for I have sinned. . .

I come now, repentant, listening:
clinking of stone currency
offered up for collection,
familiar rustle of hymnal waves.

Beer bottles once broken on deck
are forgiven, worn smooth
like rosary beads between your fingers.

I find teacup handles, plate edges,
washed up on shore,
remnants of some ship's
civilization heaved and cracked
by your wrath.

We forget what water can do
until brought to our knees by
a hurricane, baptized by flood.

Do as I Say

Howard Brown

Wrath, the outward manifestation of that
anger which has been smoldering within,
the moment when, at long last, one erupts
and begins to seek retribution for whatever
wrongs they've suffered.

But, didn't Jesus, in a fit of righteous
indignation, overturn the tables of the money
changers and drive them from the temple?

And exactly what sort of celestial tit-for-tat
was God meting out when he changed Lot's
disobedient wife into a pillar of salt?

So, at the risk of blasphemy, tell me: doesn't
this fifth of the so-called 7 Deadly Sins begin
to remind you of nothing so much as the old,
self-serving *do as I say, not as I do* spiel we
got from our parents back when we were kids?

The Incident

Matthew Horsfall

boxed anger is released
shifting loyalties in all directions
the weather reports from poor southern suburbs:
tension risen on hot rumours of defection
sliding, a living serpent
writhing in the wrath of ugly girls
sidewind and baying
bloodthirsty students learning
that violence is indeed prince of this world.

a white-hot minute
of four straight and five kicks crooked
her violent heart throbbing
with nothing left to lose once first fist hits
strips of mascara in child's socket eye
screaming for help drowning
in a sea of schadenfreude
smart phones filming
as ones and zeroes spread throughout the world.

child sacrifice,
rain in the desert.

After Wrath of Storm

Lucy Tyrrell

Here
at dawn
after wind,
incessant rain—
washout of asphalt
roads with yellow striping.
Trees that once towered tall, brave,
gently swayed with singing bird nests,
wore quivers of green, held their ground—now
toppled with frayed limbs, fallen warriors.

Mid-
morning
on Squirrel
Hill, they gathered
there in sacred space,
wearing nests of black cloth.
Storm of hatred toppled frayed
Tree of Life—incessant shooting,
rain of bullets. Lips quiver for brave,
fallen yellow stars, hold their ground, singing.

Eternal Recurrence and So On and So Forth

Michaeleen Kelly

Many short-change Nietzsche's idea of eternal recurrence,
that whatever happens will happen again and again.
They want to make it reasonable, useful, upbeat.
More like what Kant and Confucius were saying
Only doing what you could want everyone else to be doing.
Would you like it?
Somebody crapping on your shoes?
Running off with your girlfriend?

Nietzsche was never that accommodating.
Every cheek turned away from a slap
gets to be slapped again,
followed automatically by a duck or another cheek twist.
Speed up the tape
and it resembles the movements of a Rock-'em Sock-'em toy.

What Nietzsche didn't notice
was the infinite number of differences
among these inveterate sluggers
carrying out their dismal destinies as enemies,
each of their hardened faces
awaiting grace through transformation.
Perhaps a moment of redemption
at the penultimate clarifying moment.
Like when Nietzsche having just witnessed
the beating of a horse,
fell to the ground heartbroken,
his psyche permanently damaged,
his arms wrapped tenderly around the neck of the horse.

Fallback

John Maurer

What have I fallen into?
Another truth that isn't true
Another lie I prefer for the sake of my sleep schedule
Another grave under a grave where my ancestors
are buried standing; holding rosary beads or whiskey bottles
like they know conviction without being imprisoned

What is falling out of me?
Another tooth that won't turn gold
Another miscarried fetus looking like two
white pills in a white paper cup
Blood of spectrums from my septum every time I see the future
is so much further away for I squandered it
wandering in the past

Who am I falling for?
Not someone who doesn't call anymore
For I have a different number on a different phone
I walked deep enough into hell that I realized it was heaven
So I eat my bananas at the table with my bandana angel

Who am I relying on?
Another magazine that says my poetry just doesn't fit
Like no woman has ever said to me after four days of foreplay
Another magazine that will fuck me for free
but won't buy me dinner at a diner
Smearing my line breaks like red lipstick on a cigarette filter

Lip Service

Marsha Mittman

go be independent he said
live your own life
i've brought you up to be strong
and of your own mind
   to choose how you live
   to live as you choose.
but those were just words
hollow hurting words
just lip service to life

each step outside the box
the oh so narrow box
scrutinized, criticized, questioned, condemned
each foray into new territory
blasted with disapproval
so that the life she chose to live
a joyful expanding life
ultimately became a battlefield
if it didn't precisely mimic his so small life

and until the very end
the very painful end
he still mouthed from a dissipated gaunt
already dead face with hollow dead eyes
  choose how you live
  live how you choose
i've brought you up to be independent
i've brought you up to be strong
even after all his wrath
she did what he advised
and lived her own life
instead of replicating his

because he feared what he couldn't understand
and hated what she learned, knew, achieved
hating anything remotely different
and he despised her freedom
freedom he never had nor took
and he despised his inability to control her
his inability to imprison her in his oh so narrow box
ultimately fearing her joyous freedom
  because she as woman chose to live as she chose

I am so mad I

MaKayla Allen

Feel strangled to write otherwise

A lot of emotion finds synonym in another type:
Frustration to silence
Sadness to exhaustion
Futility to rage....

The emotion of silence is the atmosphere of flowers
knitted into the skirt of the skyline,
Lifting dirt off the building tops
and falling in a smoke like lace.

I ask myself to love things, and disgrace
myself in the same self-condemned way.

Constantly no one is watching, and always
I am angry in the face of anyone who finally is

I am under the weight of things
only present in the lace-scape
of the clouds with the stockings, and the
sky peppered with smoke drapes

And feel strangled by the fabrics
falling
and landing constant atop my head.

Left Cross

Robert Beveridge

She dashes her necklace
to the blacktop
between yellow lines,
follows it. Bruises
her belly
against the concrete curb,
cradles a skinned knee
below uniform Stewart plaid.

Echoes of a slammed
cathedral door. Useless
as the fool behind it,
against the trees.

Sticky dark against her thighs she
weeps rocks performs epileptic
dances to call Erzuli, Anubis,
anyone who might have helped her
recall those things she knew
before Catechism class:
dead is dead, alive is alive,
collars may be blue or white
but never lambskin.

Revenge

Jeff Santosuosso

To eat the vulture's egg
would complete his black journey.
He heisted it barehanded
from the dried birch whitened worse
than bare bones picked over bleaching.
Its fledgling sister, terrified, hissed and vomited
what her mother had vomited into her beak
from bare bones picked over bleaching
to sustain her.
Protein rushed down his throat
like a quahog,
slobbering albumen sleeve wiping
splashdown in stomach acid.

Leavenworth Penitentiary

Jemshed Khan

Out of the smoke came locusts upon the earth, and power was given them,
as scorpions of the earth have power. —Revelations 9:3

Outside the window, swarms whiten the sun,
strip branches, blot morning sky. The ground crawls.

He steps into the yard at dusk. Air buzzes with wing and jaw.
With racket in hand he swats under the basketball court light.

Thwunk, thwunk, thwunk. Forehand, backhand, spike.
Locusts drop around him until he is satisfied.

At night he hears them knock against siding,
kamikaze windows, and plunk the gutters.

When he tells the circle, the therapist takes him aside,
Practice thinking before you speak. Breathe deep. Uncurl your fists.

Later, she lays out ink blots, *There are no wrong answers.*
Tell me what you see. She smiles distantly.

Hands flat on her desk, he sighs before he speaks:
I see back to 1895. A plague blacked the sun.

Many Kansans died. Her lip curls in satisfaction
as she carefully writes, *Parole Denied.*

Then the voice of the Lord roars inside his head.
When the darkness lifts he is standing, she is dead.

Caught Out

Emily O'Sullivan

I'm angry and irritable.
Annoyed and frustrated.
I can't believe I was that stupid.

I thought I could cheat.
I was mistaken.
I got caught.

I regret my decision.
I'm truly sorry.
It wasn't worth it.

It still hurts.
The pain is agonizing.
I only have myself to blame.

I shouldn't have yelled.
It didn't help my situation.
Or mend my actions.

I have to suffer the consequences.
It will teach me.
To never forget sunscreen.

The Pompous Twit Wrote:

Karla Linn Merrifield

Amanda doesn't have the fortitude
to reply. Yeah, right. For now.
So she's worked her husband
into an email frenzy on her mad behalf
to slay her pixilated demons
She's labored to double her rage.
Plenty of fortitude yet for anger.
Plenty enough strength yet for fear.
But how soon her hard-drive falters
toward a crash. Like anyone with Intel
inside, she has nourished her neuroses
and fed on them in her viral heart
until overloaded, circuits shot,
she shuts down for the final time.

Her ego cannot hold. The machine
unplugs, every gigabyte lost.

Rosh Hashannah / Election Day

Charles Rammelkamp

I don't doubt the English translation
of the Hebrew verses in the High Holy Days *Mahzor*,
but still my jaw dropped when I read them.

"God is patient, holding back wrath.
We believe it is difficult to arouse God's fury."

What?
God always comes off as a thin-skinned bully to me,
smiting the hell out of people just because he can.
"I am a jealous god," he is always warning
and always seems to fly off the handle
at the slightest provocation,
like a third world dictator
with his face all over the postage stamps.
Because he is "God,"
whatever he does is the very definition of "right."

Imagine electing this kind of thin-skinned schmuck
for president, a bully-tyrant who picks on
weaker people just because he can –
women, Hispanics, immigrants, Muslims, the disabled –
people who don't praise him
for the sheer fact of his existence.

Now *that* would be a crime,
that would *really* piss *me* off.

The next thing that I saw

Piet Nieuwland

Woke up, it was a Chelsea morning, and the first thing that I
heard
Were crickets singing in the sun and soft breeze rustling
through the leaves

With an apricot tree to plant later on, and breakfast full of
peaches
We walked on down the road, with eggs in hand
For neighbours going to the beaches

The first thing that we saw, were bottles, plastic bags and trash
All along the roadside, plastic stuff, drink cans, and fast food
wrappers

There was junk and rubbish, metal rods and bolts, more bottles
Cars in pieces, pieces of cars, more cans, plastic bags and
polystyrene boxes

There was filthy old clothing, smashed up TVs, bed frames and
broken fridges
The next thing that I saw, was a stylish grey ladies boot, or so I
thought
It was instead on closer look, a big fat greyish tongue, sweaty
fresh,
lying in the morning sun.

A *Bos taurus* tongue licking at me looking at you I asked it
How did you get there, must have fallen off the back of truck?

A kilogram it weighed, or thereabouts and thirty three centi-
meters long it was
From rough dexterous tip to blackish calloused patch deep in
the throat

Well, we did pick it up, put it in our handy egg bag, to take
home
To make a chicken duck 'n tongue stew, with a few spuds 'n
onions too.

You didn't believe I did that did you, no! Well yes we did, we
picked it up
Took it home, gave it to the chooks who scoffed it, they just
scoffed it down

So when we go walking along the road, to keep an eye out what
is there
We might find something that is yours, and is that fair?

Don't throw your rubbish from out your car window
Don't let it fall off the back of your truck
Don't tip it on the roadside verge

You might be in luck, but then again
You will make us really really angry
All that trash needs somewhere to go
And it might all just come right back at you

Headline: *Woman stops cops from beating her son*

Shawn Aveningo-Sanders

Hell hath no wrath like a mother
protecting her child,
her son crouched down
at the feet of men
with guns.

The madness in her eyes,
rage fiery as her scarlet sash,
veins popping in her forearm,
she holds steady the machete
at his Adam's apple.

> *Don't you dare move.*
> *Don't you dare shoot*
> *my boy.*
> *What he do to you?*
> *He done nothing wrong.*
> *Maybe he reach in his pocket.*
> *Maybe he look sideways*
> *grin*
> *in a way that make you feel—*
> *uncomfortable*

unsafe. How safe
you feel now?
guns wielded in this
circle jerk you call
the law. No bluff, sir.
You shoot my boy, I cut you.
Simple as dat.

Blue lights fade.
Sirens stop.
Guns holstered.

That's right. You best
be on your way. Ain't nothin'
to see here. Git. Go on now.
Leave us be.

Unwelcome Visitor

Rick Blum

If-Only barged in last night, settling on the couch
like an old college buddy planning to crash
for a few days … or weeks, if you're not lucky.

Why are you here? I asked.

"Because you decided to order pizza rather than cook
dinner," he said chortling at my question
like it was a Seinfeld punch line.

But I like pizza, and cooking's getting tiresome.

"Sure," he sighed. "Only this time that seemingly innocuous
decision resulted in the delivery guy ringing your doorbell,
which compelled the dog to maniacally jump off the couch
onto the slick hardwood floor, where his right hind leg
slipped out awkwardly from beneath him, thus tearing
his ACL and condemning your wife to eight weeks
of lugging around 25 pounds of dead weight."

*But he jumps off the couch all the time. My decision
to order pizza and his injury were only
connected by happenstance!*

"That's true. Yet that won't stop you from irately
grumbling my name several times a day while I snack
on your guilt – until the dog's back to chasing rabbits,
and your wife's sore back eases up enough
to resume pleasurable evening activities."

Can't you just hang out for a few hours this one time,
then go back to wherever you dwell between calamities,
leaving me in peace?

"Of course, I can," he said as an oleaginous smile formed
in one corner of his mouth. "Just learn to control
your wrath every time life proves beyond your control."

Well, that doesn't sound too hard.

"If only, my friend. If only."

Lo-Fiction

Judah Eli

Sakura-tinted glasses
That reveal you in the rain,
Watch:
Back of bus,
Hydroxide-blue in shapes
And fabric pigments,
Snapshot shapes adjust the
Pigments
Without window seats,
The morning, flash
The moments wrapped in plastic,
Flash
The moments, wrath
And all the plastic
Speak in words of entropy,
Hydroxy, bleeding, entropy
In moments, doldrum colour:
Snapshot
Space-girl with the crackshot
Driving
Fog along the highway flash
And goalposts in the dark.
Speak: words that make them dark,
Flash, eyes and earlobes film-grain tracing laugh-lines in the

dark.
Neat.
Touches the lips, the
Train-mirror
Drips
With vapoury rain with
Plastic between
To cool the rumbling of the sexual machine.
The ignition.
The obscene
Firing
Of cock-and-ball pistons
Against flesh.
Misfire.
Echoes without them,
Stratosphere weeks,
Armpits sweat
And perfume reeks
Your art placenta
Heaving with an
U
L
T
R
A
S
I
L
E
N
T

D
E
A
T
H
C
R
Y

In the evening.
Reclaim your youth with violence,
Trip existential balls,
Overbear your body with the movement of your soul,
Hear the earth turn beneath your feet
Entrench your persona in myth
Erupt chaotically into your own narrative without a single
regard for character, point of view or setting
And cherish every last memory of your human metamorphosis.
Even now
I remember how
Her skin smelt like glycerine hibiscus,
The night her grandmother read
My fortune.
How she told me who I am and
All that time,
She sat right there beside me at the
Table.
Although I do not realise things will
End

So much quicker than they
Begin,
This
Moment
Is
Art.
In this moment
I am the god of light and music,
And all the words are none.

Nature's Cycle

Colleen Moyne

Mother Nature
is in a mood today.
She is banging on the doors
and crying outside my window,
but I dare not let her in.

Like a spoilt child
she is throwing tantrums
tossing bins around the yard,
tipping chairs
and pulling washing off the line

Her tempestuous ranting
has sent the dog
scurrying under the bed.

Nothing will allay her anger,
no-one can calm her,
and so… we wait
until, tired and spent,
she sleeps

Were she flesh and blood
some might ask,
'That time of the month?'
But no –
That time of the year.

a striking world strikes at your core with a vengeful whore

Geralda Gjomakaj

with tepid temperatures and still air
you feel the brew on your skin and your buzzing arm hair
you've heard it before it cracks the grown
like a whip that's left your skin bruised and brown
in the open I admire the electric feel it unleashes with its wrath,
subordinate to its power I sink to its mercy and beg forgiveness
for my heresy,
in surrender I lay vulnerable,
so lightning struck me and all my pieces came undone
that's what it felt like when I found out what you had done

(Potato) Wrath

Shane Guthrie

There was no space
Between action and reaction
What I said was
"Why are you doing that, dear?"
But I may as well have been spitting fire, melting the carpet
Around her feet

I don't know what she said back but I responded
"To. Your. Room!"
While I cleaned up in a rage
The world burned down to a tiny spot
Of potatoes ground into a carpet

With the mess cleaned up
I began to see the rest of the house
Messy but undamaged
I started to hear sniffling from behind her door
She was crying
And I was changing
Out of my dragon scales

On Second Thought

Ron. Lavalette

I had to bite my tongue. I
had to bite my tongue and
count to ten. Slowly. I had to
take a few deep breaths and
count to ten eight times.
It was all I could do. I barely
managed to zip my lip, keep
my cool—

      —no, wait a minute;
that's not how it happened.
I had no real cool to keep;
I guess I let my unzipped lip
remain unzipped; I guess
I bit my tongue to no avail,
bit my tongue and squeezed
the trigger, counting the rounds
and the bodies as they fell.

Study in Red

George Yatchisin

Those irked, tired lines
across your eyes
are like blood-red macaw
blurs across the sky
in the lone place where
we haven't killed or caged them.

They are too noble for us,
too willing to color the air,
too quick to express
their soul-curdling call
having nothing to do with their beauty.

Sure, shoot them down for silence
for all that's wrong in the world.

Chainsaw Massacre

Martin Christmas

The instrument of Death is spied,
then bought, and loaded
in the boot. No strip search,
police car siren, ASIO report,
just loaded in the boot,
with anticipation of what murder
lay ahead.

'Read the instructions carefully,'
the manual said. I did, I did, I did
again, until in fear,
I set aside my task, my deadly task,
and father confessed to Facebook
friends who warned me of
electrocution, decapitation,
wrathful kickback, not the political kind,
but chainsaw hitting obstacle wrath, and going
for the jugular, not wood, my head.
An avalanche of fears released.

Step one was done, and then step two,
involving putting on the chain.
Almost sweated blood to make the
job as good as poss, so that
injury or death (mine),
didn't happen on my watch.

Then an inner voice yelled,
'Do it now!
Don't put it off till after lunch.'
And donning goggles, ear protectors, work gloves,
gum boots, and looking like an
astronaut or some weird ghoul,
I began the task, the bloody task itself.

Set the instrument of Death in place;
filled the oil sump; connected cable
from the house; hooked in the extension cord;
took a safe position on flat ground.

Prepare to meet thy doom!

The innocent tree stump
lay silent just ahead and unaware its
cutting fate. The old hand saw
bemoaned its loss of kingship in the shed.

One final check of printed words;
turned on the power; three deep breaths;
pressed the red button.
The instrument of Death alive,
fast rips into the screaming wood.
The chainsaw massacre commenced.

Fifteen minutes of total fearful focus,
concentration, following instruction
imprinted in my head,
cutting with abandon, cactus wood,
whatever came my way.

Chainsaw virginity is lost.
Orgasmic pleasure moment,
dripping sweat,
such macho primitive release.

An end for now. Enough.
Lunchtime, but thinking,
'If I were more unhinged,
I might search out more deadly
cut and thrust.'

This chainsaw massacre stuff
is fun.

I only lost
three fingers

and a thumb!

Divided

Melisa Quigley

Baby crying
milk dried up
you sit drinking
swearing,
slurring words
sick child
screaming
and kicking
hard to control
you take the
top off another
oblivious to it all
heart ripped out
on a butcher's hook
wanting to leave
obligated to stay
not knowing what to do
in a big rage
rent due
no money to pay
yelling and cussing
wishing I were
dreaming
and upon waking
you would
all go away

A Night with Cerberus, 1982

Pegi Deitz Shea

The Plaka, Athens.
Jody meets a rich man,
makes dinner plans.
"Be careful," I say.
She doesn't return that night.
Nor the next morning.
Nor the next afternoon.
No messages—no signal!
We are due in Corfu.
Mad, worried, I spill my story
at our cheap hotel bar.

At dinner break, the bartender says, "You must eat. My friend
has restaurant."
I shrug. "Okay." We walk to a car. I didn't know there would
be a car.
The kebab is savory, the couscous fluffy, spanakopita tangy.
He talks a lot. "My mother, no school, my sister, no school."
"What do they do all day?" I ask.
"They clean, they cook. Me, I want to go America, make bar,
make rich."

He insists on paying our bill. "I need clothes at home. Work all night,

open bar for breakfast."

The car careens through a labyrinth. I'm dizzy, disoriented.

Finally he parks. "Come. Only minute."

"I'll wait here," I say.

"No safe. No lights."

My stomach tight, I huff. "Okay. Only a minute."

I follow him up three flights. He unlocks his door, saying, "Come."

"No, I'll wait here."

"Only minute. Come."

I back away. "I'm staying here."

His eyes go olive black.

Grunting, he grabs me,
pulling me inside. "No! Ohxi! No!"
I kick, "Ohxi!" I punch. "Stop! Help! ...Fire! Fotia!"
Two doors fly open down the hall.
Neighbors peer at me, growl at him.
He drops my arms, yells at me, "Go hotel self."
He slams his door.
I stifle a sob. "Where am I?"
The neighbors shrug,
shut their doors.

A bus shelter two blocks away. I wait. Cars crawl by, men invite me for rides.

Finally a bus. I hold out drachma. "Go Omonia Square?"

The driver shakes his head.

I point all over my map. "Where am I?"

He blows the hair off his brow. Voices rise behind him. Men stand, lean out

the window, leer. The bus is capsizing. The driver scolds the
passengers. The bus untilts. He beckons me on board, points to
the open seat across the aisle. The bus is full of men, only men.
At a big intersection, the driver turns right. The men holler,
motioning left.
The driver argues back. Eyes stab the back of my head.
A few blocks later, he pulls to a stop. Sweeps me to the door.
"To Omonia."
I offer drachma again. He shakes his head. I thank him. He
turns the bus around.

Two buses later, one o'clock, Omonia Square. Café sidewalks
full of men. They drool, catcall, loll their tongues. I put my
head down, stream through stinging cigar smoke, hear the
word "bitch".

I plow up Athinas. My lodestar, the Acropolis, lit acid green.
My decrepit pension,
a speck at its feet. Oh.... Footsteps echo stark. Following me?
"No," I tell the dark, "just a tourist. Relax." Footsteps closer,
harder, hammering. Now something panting. Brute shoulders
shove me to my knees, stalk past me, hulk down my street. Shit!
Pocketknife pointed, I hurry straight instead on Athinas.
He jeers, "American girl, look!"
Sideways, slit-eyed: *Sick!*
Teeth grind. Full steam ahead.
Mind unleashes:

You pig! You filth!
Follow me again and I'll slice it off!
How dare you? Do you have
mother wife sister daughter
who only cook only clean? Do you

wag your dick at them?
Do you have sons dreaming
to be like you when they grow up?
Stick it down your throat, choke and die!

Suddenly French words somewhere—two women walk toward
me. I beg, "*S'il vous plait, un homme me suit. Pouvez-vous marcher avec
moi à mon pension?*"
"*Bien sur.*"
When we round my corner, the animal is still flashing.
The French women laugh loudly, point. "*Oo la la! Exhibitionist!
Quel petit cyclops! Si petit comme ca!*" Their fingers measure an inch
of air.

Alone, I lock myself in my room. Tears sear my stupidity.

Jody returns the next morning with tales of yachting and
champagne.
"You should have been there!" she says.
I give her the finger, don't speak civil to her for days.
She apologizes. We pledge
not to leave each other alone again.

Prosaic Paradox Given POTUS 40s Alzheimer's

Gerard Sarnat

Particularly since Governor Reagan
closed poor people's in-patient facilities
but didn't fund outpatient services
California's had mental health problems.

But like cancer (which remains a killer),
we aren't terribly good stewards
of our cultural (each man for his-herself
impersonal even cutthroat cities)

and physical (toxins galore) environments
that fuel huge front-end diseases,
only some of which can perhaps be treated.
Ditto for cardiovascular illnesses

which low-cost fast-food/cigarettes increase
destruction to those underclasses
plus, also become prevalent in Asia and Africa
while those of us with the means

to access to life-style changes well as healthcare
do quite well thank you very much.
Anybody remembers RD Laing, the revolutionary
Scotch psychiatrist back in the 60s

who wrote "madness" was an appropriate adaptive
response to our society? In my decades
caring for homeless etc., this often synergized with
substances plus AIDS as a triple threat.

Wise Words Without Wrath Will Win:
A Tertiary Abecedarian

Ken Gosse

Kind words, aptly shared—welcome help from the wise—
will oft be a fair breeze against angered replies
as it cools heated souls when their temperatures rise,
so they don't lose their heads or lose sight of the prize
which is everyone's—not yours; that falsehood belies—
but as food which is offered to gaunt, hungry eyes;
for the goodness of man is not just in what lies
in the heart, but in deed, as each one of us tries
to make inroads of hope, seeing how love applies
as we join, hand-in-hand, heart-in-heart, we apprise
that the knowing is good, but the sowing implies
that we're like one another, though different in guise,
and our minds will confirm what our hearts realize:
that it's never too late to help those whose demise
might our own boat, humanity, cause to capsize,
for each person, including the ones we despise
form a quantum of life which we can't analyze,

but just rolling the dice will come up with snake eyes
and our safety in numbers is just a disguise
for not taking account of those we ostracize,
and so under those auspices which should chastise
when we vent in our anger against non-allies,
then may we, bound in unity, find our reprise
not like xerophytes, thirstless, yet growing in size,
but in yearning to love one another, likewise.
At our zenith, like stars, may we brighten our skies.

The Player

Tony Daly

He jumps, kicks, twitches,
is taut, tense, intense,
feels every hit, cut, blast,
as finger vibrations announce gut punches
that batter heart strings.

Admonitions of, *gosh, golly*,
and *what the fudge*
express innocent hostility
before the guttural *NOOOOO!*
as a Creeper strikes down
his blocky alter ego.

The wireless remote
skitters across the floor,
sending memories spiraling to younger self
slicing enemies with gun-swords,
blasting slimes with fireballs,
commanding gods with frantic button clicks,
but when an enemy struck fatally before a save point,
so many remotes exploded against the wall.

Their eviscerated innards
collapsing along the edges of battle
to join the objects of wrath:
fast food containers, notebooks,
soda bottles, pizza boxes, dirty clothes.

Kneeling before my son,
soothing wild eyes that
seek vengeance through
destruction of infinite digital lives,

Come back to me boy.
Don't let the darkness take you.

The Gaps

Corey Mesler

"There's no one left between myself and me." Julien Baker

We all believe in the gaps,
the spaces between
you and me.
There are stations of the
crossed. There
are those still angry about
the conflagration.
To be public, to have a
personality, seems
such a burden, it's a wonder
anyone bothers.
No one bothers. I write this
from my garret,
where fresh straw is a treat.
Maybe tomorrow
I will see you
on the street. I will be the
man wearing your
face as a mask. You'll just
be you, the
last woman I could ever love.

Piece Me Together

Ben Pitts

I know there are fragments
of my father's wrath in me—
tough-love
gift wrapped in a sheen of told-you-sos
as you spill milk on the floor.
At the right angle, does my hand
seem wide enough to smother
the sun and all the sky?

His did
       on its way
       upward.

I'm trying to remember that pit
in my stomach as I ask you
to find a towel and clean up
this mess.

If I ever send you to your room
holding yourself together
please hold up a mirror
to my face so I can see
my father's black hair
tumbling down my shoulders.

Country

Roberta Gould

It's anti-song
They shut you down
And if you're good
You get a Home
A face to freak
Your troubles to
A plate to eat
Your vittles from
Otherwise
Be still
Don't butt into private
Conversations
Keep your eyes on
Your own feet
Be careful!
independent
individual
and not too friendly

One by one
you'll March behind
a flag that thrills
as no God can
Up high it stirs
in Friday's breeze
Smile and thank
Your lucky stars
please

Dear Editor

Carl 'Papa' Palmer

I received a cookie cutter form letter of rejection from the editor for someone else's poem in my SASE. That someone else sent me the acceptance letter she received for my poem in her SASE.

My poetic response: this seventeen syllable "precursory curse" villanelle.

Dear Editor,

I appreciate the time you took to send this rejection letter
about your decision not to publish me or put my work in print,
but I think, indeed, you really need to do your rejections better.

With your fine job title I felt you'd be the writing standard setter
'til you rejected me in an SASE someone else had sent.
Should I appreciate the time you took on this rejection letter?

My intent is not to anger or put my future chance in fetter,
nor is the matter of this patter solely to chastise you or vent,
yet I think, indeed, you really need to make your rejections better.

Some of my best saved rejections have never fed a paper shredder;
that's how I detect, in retrospect, rhyme and reason to circumvent
the monumental task you took to construct this rejection letter.

Try to get the right writer's name in your rejection letter header
or you may wonder where the submissions for your next edition went.
So I think, indeed, you really need to sort your rejections better.

In closing, I'll just make this point I surely hope you will consider:
Always remember you cannot edit what we writers never sent.
Though I appreciate the time you took on your rejection letter,
still I think, indeed, you really need to check your rejections better.

Yours Truly,
Carl 'Papa' Palmer ~ writer

Mrs. God

Alan Walowitz

When sick and tired of prayers ignored,
in my long encounter with our boorish lord,
I call upon the one who wedded old I Am.
(Not empty-headed Maryam
who was in truth no innocent, liked to flaunt
her ascetic ways, at least in the account
I've got, wine-induced, direct from the Mrs.
who when sobered up, usually dismisses
such rumors, but when generously lubed
can make trouble at home, or in markets abroad.)

Mrs. God can remember, Where the hell's the remote?
Mrs. God can figure out what tie might work
with that god-awful shirt.
Mrs. God can cook up a storm
when the boss drops by unexpected.
And when Mr. Bluster beats his chest,
claims vengeance is mine,
and starts in to curse like a sailor,
she soothes him with a simple,
Why don't we talk about it first?

Sometimes this works.

Politezza

Michael Estabrook

Waiting for my wife on a quiet bench
outside the dress shop,
the sun warming my face,
when an older man sits down next to me.
He's on his cellphone of course:
"Yes Leslie, it's a shame about Sean.
No we didn't get to see them this time out.
You're so kind to say that. Give my love to Shitface..."

No they will not be even a little discrete,
will not stop blaring out their inanities
for our miserable delectation,
show no consideration, no decorum, nada zip niente.
I begin to look around for a brick
or a nice smooth stone
with enough heft for me to crush
this fucking guy's skull
with one swift spatterless blow.

If Only You Knew

Sara Abend-Sims

If only you knew what it's like
I tried to hush her yelling
gave her a civilized smile
her words loud and sticky
clung when I passed her by
gnawed at me when I crossed
the square's traffic lights

was it the colour of her skin
the half empty bottle by her feet?
she didn't look too old
hair on the scruffy side orange top
and bare toes peeping out
index finger thrusting condemnation
her aura crackling hissing rage

I passed her by like all others
hurried ready to almost fly
if only you knew what it's like
if only I i-tuned my ears
pretend she didn't exist
keeping at bay hushing and smiles
her wrath would not have come my way

when next in Victoria Square
will I pass by blind-mute
will I offer no solace won't even try
or will I stay by her side
disregarding green lights
and then
will I find out?

Ezekiel Smith,

on Seeing John Sprockett in the Camp of Captain William Quantrill: Kansas 1863

Robert Cooperman

'Til he muttered his name, I thought a monster
had rose from the grave, his face ripped
by that grizzly him and that Pawnee dispatched:
its skeleton moth-white when we rode
into their camp, Sprockett healed up best
as he'll ever be, but his face forever a nightmare,
though I try not to wince at the sight of him.

I remember him from back home, the minister's
stepson; he beat the Preacher to death
after that man of God killed Sprockett's Ma
for a whore, though I heard she never traipsed
about after they was yoked, though that made
no never mind to Preacher, perched so high
in Heaven, only Jesus was above him.

At first, I thought to warn the Captain not
to trust Sprockett: an outsider, and maybe
that gouging hiding an Abolitionist spy.
But when I heard his name, I knew him
for one of us, and when he testified the Injun
had saved his life, good enough for me.

From what I hear about how he sent to hell
those men seeking to avenge the Preacher,
I know he's badger-fierce when we'll hit
Lawrence like a twister. And that he didn't
join in dirtying the farm wife and her daughter
on our first raid, whilst others jumped on them,
whooping like at a river baptism,
why that speaks to his good character.

It hurt my soul we had to shoot them, but Federals
had murdered our women in that jail collapse
they claimed was an accident. Accident, my foot!

Not on a Tuesday

Elizabeth Buttimer

This is not my day to die
he says as he stares down
the barrel of a gun to the face
of the woman aiming it at him.
You don't want to do this,
there's not a good ending
if you choose this path.

She says nothing but her hand
begins to shake imperceptibly,
at first and then, the wobble
takes over, and her eyes redden.
We can still work this out, find
a solution, it doesn't have to end
this way.

He begins slowly moving closer
to her, to the barrel, to the choice
she would have to make and what
he'd have to do to counter
that decision. Like a kitten, his
words so soft, like tiny paws
of stealth, they creep into the crevices
of her brain and crawl into her heart.
Soothing words pour like honeyed tea
down a raging throat, until the rage
rises again like battery acid.

She doesn't want to back down, yet
she doesn't know how it came to this.
Their locked eyes hold position.
Give me the gun,
he says without a waver.
You need to give me the gun, now.
She pauses and lets the gun roll flat
in her hand. His hand pounces
for the weapon, never moving a step
closer to her, never breaking eye contact.
It'll be alright, we can work something out,
he says to the heaving jangle of nerves.

Facing Danger after 9/11

Mark Hudson

Shortly after 9/11, a friend and I were coming out of a place in Highland Park, Illinois, where there was a huge seven eleven. There was a man outside washing the windows, which was weird, it was ten o'clock at night.

Some teenagers drove by, and my friend waved and said, "Hey, how's it going?"

Their response was to curse us out and throw a giant bottle of soda at us. (We suspect they were drunk.) So my friend impulsively threw a rock at the car, and it hit the car, and they got out and started chasing us.

I had just quit smoking, so I couldn't run that fast. The teen was chasing me. I slipped and fell on some train tracks. The teen laughed, and I picked myself up, and my friend and I hid behind a dumpster in the alley.

We got in my friend's van and
escaped. The next week we came back,
and the window washer was there again.
He said he saw the whole thing, and he
wrote down their license plate numbers.
He somehow looked their names up,
and they had "middle-eastern sounding
names," which made everybody paranoid
right after 9/11.

He said to my friend, "You should
press charges," but my friend said, "No,
I think I'll just forget about it."
I realize how long ago that was
by now, and the world at large continues
to become a dangerous place to live.

Wrath of Biblical Proportion

Ruth Sabath Rosenthal

the wrath of Ishmaelites and Israelites alike —
all begotten from two sons of Abraham —
half brothers, Ishmael and Isaac, whose fate
spawned a fractured brotherhood far surpassing
Cain and Abel. Two halves of one bottomless well
of familial blood ever-coursing with a vengeance
throughout the world: The familial life force

of civilians, politicians, terrorists, soldiers,
children — all scanning the horizon
beyond the scope of the Garden of Eden
in the land flowing with milk & honey
and the ceaseless flood of bad blood rising
and spreading like wildfire far and wide,
generation after generation — no end in sight.

Familial blood of today's kin to Ishmael
1st son of Abraham — his Islamic brood —
the Koran they revere
hijabs & kaffiyehs
their religious wear
the ghusi
they cleanse themselves in.

Familial blood of today's kin to Isaac
2nd son of Abraham — his Hebrew brood —
the Talmud they revere
sheitels & yarmulkes
their religious wear
the mikveh
they cleanse themselves in.

O, that each of us — all descendants Ishmaelites
and Israelites, would comprehend that
the word *God* in any language translates as
the God of Abraham and of his 1st wife Sarah,
mother of Isaac; and in time, the God of Hagar,
Sarah's maidservant and Abraham's concubine
(later wife #2) mother of Ishmael.

Mother and son banished because of Sarah's jealousy
and fear. That banishment, turning Hagar and Ishmael
away from the God of Abraham. The exile
and the reasons for it, very likely, the genesis of
The Straw that Broke the Camel's Back and sticking point
of any peace-making negotiations worldwide
since God knows when.

Footnote:
Familial Blood, traced through Talmudic and Midrashic literature and pre-
Hebrew scriptures, is the blood shared by Adam's progeny. In those documents,
Lilith was *Adam's* 1st wife & *Eve* his 2nd, which opens up a whole can of worms this
poet can't see clear to sort out here. That *Lilith* doesn't appear in the Qur'an, but *Eve*
does (as *Hawwa, Adam's* only wife) doesn't change the fact that *Ishmaelites* & *Israelites*
shared in Adam's bloodline and, thus, so do we (*the global we*) today!

Dearest Bastard

Lisa Rhodes-Ryabchich

You have finally done it this time!
Pushed me over the edge—
saw me standing there wavering
unsure and unsettled, hair all a muss,
and teeth unbrushed.
My breath is rancid with rage;
the garlic has caught my tummy on fire!
I'm the last dancer
on this mad merry-go-round, and I'm tired
of being pushed around!
You've offered me the door, the cold
indiscreet divorce—
now here is the *coffin birth*
you've wanted for so long—
you might as well have planned it yourself!
I've done everything to please you—
birthed your child, paid for your school—
the wedding—the rings, even invited
your gruesome sisters for dinner during the holidays.
Now I have finished listening to your weary sad tale
of *marital blues* and I'm done!
Go ahead you *cowardly Bastard*
give yourself a hearty pat on the back.

Prose

Prose

Hardback

Edward O'Dwyer

I'm an avid reader, having grown up in a home full of books. Ever since I was a little girl I have been devouring them, with dreams of one day writing one of my own.

My ex-boyfriend, when we were together, used to joke around about me preferring books to people. It was true, of course, but I always ignored him, kept reading.

When he confessed to sleeping with other women, he said I'd made it too easy. He said it could have gone on forever, and that I'd never have caught him, even if it was going on and I was in the room, because if I was, my head would probably be stuck far too intently in a book anyway.

All I had in my hand at the time he came clean was a paperback edition, and so I smacked him with it repeatedly as best I could, letting out my anger. It wasn't very effective. I was fairly sure he wouldn't even have a mark to show for it.

If I'd spent the extra few quid I'd have had the hard copy of it in my hand and would surely have done a bit more damage, but that's hindsight for you. I always buy the hardback now, of course, just in case there's a next time.

Bang and Blame

Michael Webb

I have an ID hanging around my neck that says I belong here, but I am an interloper. There is a long row of reclining chairs in this room, each one surrounded by equipment and IV setups and single, sad televisions broadcasting silently, separated by institutional striped curtains that don't reach the floor. I walk down the row, trying not to look, but catching enough of a glance to know which one she is in. A man with gray hair snores in one, the earbud that has fallen broadcasting the tinny, measured speech of a newscast. Her chair is at the end of the row. I know it's her, there aren't that many people named Siobhan in this world.

She doesn't look the way I remember. Her face is drawn, the skin on her collarbones tight where they emerge from the sweatshirt she is wearing. She has a Brooklyn Dodgers baseball cap on, but it is obvious that she has little hair underneath it. She is turned onto her side, a blanket pulled up to her chin, her eyes shut tight, like a child trying not to see a scary movie. I think about leaving, letting her be, but I am cemented to the spot. When I have made up my mind to leave, she opens her eyes, then turns slightly to look at me. Her eyes are still enormous, hazel like a cat's. They have more wrinkles now, but they are the same eyes.

"You," she says, her voice rough. I move towards the glass of water on the table beside her.

"Don't bother," she says, and reaches behind her, takes the cup, and sips from the straw. "It doesn't help. But it makes them happy that I drink. So I drink." She has an Irish accent, but her voice is no longer musical, now a caricature. "More importantly, though, what in the name of fuck are you doing here?"

"I work here... I saw your name on an admission, I saw, I mean, I didn't... I didn't know," I stammer. Sentences collide in my head like cars at an intersection with no traffic light.

"Jesus," she says. "Of all the gin joints..."

She lets the thought trail off, then starts again.

"You know why you didn't know? I didn't want you to know. I didn't want you to know because I'm done with you, exactly the way you were done with me back then. Leave me alone."

She lifts the cup to her lips again, and sips.

"Wait," she says, her voice still a rasp. "One more thing. You don't get to suffer about this, okay? This is mine. I was twenty when we met. Fucking twenty. Yes, an adult, blah blah blah. But goddamned twenty. I didn't know anything. You were so smart. So cool. So funny and clever with your references and your stupid little jokes. And I fell for you. Wasn't the first time, and I'm sure it wasn't the last time. I know what I look like. Well... what I looked like. I know what you like. I'm sure I was one in a series. Idealistic, young, hearts full of love songs and weakness. And then when you were done, I was yesterday's dishes. Used up. Over. You didn't care. You never cared. So you don't get to care now. You don't get to think about the beautiful girl, the eager student you used and disposed of years ago. You don't get to shed any tears over me. You didn't care then, and you don't get to care now."

She raises the water and sips again.

"Do you remember the CD you were listening to all the time that summer? The one with the bear face thing on the cover? It was orange?"

"Monster," I say, my own voice a desiccated husk. I swallow, very conscious of my own body. "R.E.M."

"I was just a bang," she says quietly. "And you get the blame."

The Undertow

Mark Crimmins

"Jimmy," she'd say, "what the hell are ya sayin? Whats this goddam *undertow* yer jabberin on about?"

And I'd tell her, "Sue, yer kin say what the hell ya likes, but yer also sayin stuff yer not even aware ya sayin. Ya aint jes sayin stuff wiv yer mouf. *Thats* what I'm talking about. *Thats* the fuckin undertow. Yer can tell me ya dont want nuthin ter do wiv me no more. Thats fine. But therez a undertow. Right when yer pushin me away wiv what yer sayin, yer pullin me right back towardz ya wiv what yer not sayin."

Well. I'll be doggone if me sayin this dint damn near git her goat so much she jes about tore out her own eyez wiv frustration. She dint like this notion she wuz sending me messinjiz she dint know she wuz sendin me. No sir. And the more I said it the more it drove her nuts. Funny thing about it wuz the more it drove her nuts the more it durn proved she wuz sendin me a undertow. She wuz pullin me towards her wiv her heart right when she wuz pushin me away wiv her mouf. Thats all I wuz tryina tell her. But no. She has to git up on her high horse and start yellin and screamin and stampin her feet like lil ole Rumpelzwhatzizname hizself.

"Jimmy, caint ya see how much I hate ya? Caint ya see how blind ya iz? Caint ya see what a piece a shit I think ya iz? I've had enough a ya Jimmy! I'm leavin ya Jimmy! Ya aint gonna see me no more Jimmy! Not till hell iz froze over and not then neither! I'm through, Jimmy, goddamit, I'm through!"

When she got goin like this I wuz alwayz struck by the rhythm of it. The way she carried on n such. It wuz almost like a song. I spoze in her own mind it wuz indeed a song. Some kinda fucked up luv song. Some sorta song a farewell. And there wuz timez when I almost believed she truly wanted to leave me be.

But there wuz both fire n ice in them blue eyez a hern. I dint jes listen at her wiv ma earz. I also heard what she wuz sayin to ma eyez. Thats how I figgered she wuz sending me mixed messinjiz. Therez the linguidge a the mouf but therez also the linguidge a the body. I wuz listenin alright. I wuz listenin real close. I wuz hearin everythin she wuz sayin loud and clear. I wuz all earz. All eyez.

But like I sez—there wuz a undertow.

Horseplay

Patience Mackarness

Diane said, "That's not physically possible."

"What isn't?" I asked. We were in the National Gallery, and the huge painting in front of us was Piero di Cosimo's 'Fight Between the Lapiths and the Centaurs'. There was a lot going on. Flying hooves, severed limbs, upset winejugs. One portly centaur had his arms round the waist of a fleeing naked woman.

"For a centaur to rape a human," Diane said. "It can't be done. Think about it." We all did.

"Everything all right, girls?" said our teacher, Mr Baines. He had heard the hysterical laughter, and had probably caught the word *rape* too. Diane had a carrying sort of voice.

We assured Mr Baines everything was fine, and bent our heads over our worksheets again. But later, at the back of the coach, the discussion continued. Diane said the centaur's human arms were too far away from its horse-dick to be useful. And without the arms, it couldn't rape anyone.

Jane, who went to riding lessons every Saturday, said she had once seen a stallion 'cover' a mare, and he had used his teeth.

"Q.E.D.," Diane said triumphantly. "A centaur doesn't *have* teeth. At least only human ones, which would be no good at all."

I pointed out that 'Fight Between the Lapiths and the Centaurs' looked like an attempted gang-bang; perhaps the centaurs had been planning to help each other out.

We talked about sex constantly in those days, although none of us had done IT yet. We were all, with the possible exception of Jane, a bit confused about the mechanics of IT. But we researched energetically, pre-internet of course. One girl had borrowed a porn mag from her brother; we thought the act looked gross. 'Lady Chatterley's Lover' made the whole thing sound more fun. Diane had started seeing a local boy, whom her parents described disapprovingly as *rough* (Diane said they meant *common*, but didn't dare say so), which should have been helpful to our investigations, but so far her dates hadn't yielded much information.

Sometimes the discussions were serious, sometimes not. "Suppose you wanted to *seduce* a centaur?" I asked in the lunch queue. "A romantic night out. What would you have for dinner?"

"Bran mash as a starter," said Jane. "Then steak and chips. An apple for dessert. And pony nuts with your coffee."

We demanded details about Diane's boyfriend. We were envious of her opportunities, awed by her nerve, and a little scared for her too.

"Is he a noble savage?" I asked, and Diane said, "No, he's a centaur."

We squealed, and insisted on knowing more.

"Well," she said, "he's big —" Shrieks. "You've got dirty minds," said Diane, with a look of false virtue. "Of course I meant *tall*. But he's also hairy—" We insisted on knowing *where* he was hairy, but all Diane would say was "he's hairy in all the places I've seen *so far*." She added primly, "And he's only got one thing on his mind."

This was quite delicious, and we continued to follow the relationship as avidly as a soap opera. But one morning, Diane came into school wearing a look of Homeric wrath.

"So?" said Jane breathlessly. "Did he ravish you like a Lapith woman?"

"He tried," said Diane shortly.

"No! What happened?"

"I kicked him in the pony nuts," said Diane, and dissolved into shaky laughter.

The Mob

Sam Cameron-McKee

I became one with the mob. We were liberated by the masks that covered our faces and choked our breathing. We were invigorated by the roar that tore and ripped at our throats. The fire had been set, we embraced it not fearing the blaze. We came together in violent intimacy, and began to burn.

I had gathered with them under the bruised clouds, the air tingling with ozone and the oppressive pressure of a storm about to be born. The horizon constrained by towers of glass and steel, ribs holding up the sky. The tarmac hot beneath my sneakered feet, pumping with the blood of urban existence. The city quaked at our step and mustered its antibodies to fight us off. They arrived, blue and silver, shining with guns and batons. They had screamed at me, threatened me; they wore their wrath as plainly as mine.

But I had paid them no mind. Their wrath was not righteous, not like mine. I had come with a singular thought:

Justice.

The reason had been lost in a sea of reasons. The woman shot last week, the child the week before, a sea of blood. The corruption exposed last month, the bribes the month before, a sea of rot. The fear, which ate away at all our minds, the thought that tomorrow might strike us with the city's misfortune – a fine, a firing, a bullet. There was no individual reason left. All that remained was a sense that something must be done, that I had sat in comfort too long. I had not – at first – thought of violence.

I had pressed forward, part of the tide, but still an individual. We were pathogens, free radicals trying to tear down the city's carefully protected silence, but we did not fight. I yelled back at the wall of blue and silver before us. They stood firm, but not proud, merely cells doing their duty. No, I wore a mask but I was proud to be there. I pressed forward, and yelled, intent on change; certain that a difference could be made without bloodshed.

Then the sound had echoed out.

I could see – as clear as the lightning which stabbed at the air – the blood. A single shot. Was it fired in haste or in caution? Was it in defence or attack? No answer could be enough. The blood stained the tarmac and it was decided.

I became one with the mob.

The screaming came first, then the pushing, then the knives. We pressed forward, but now with bloodlust. We had tried, so truly we had tried, but now every answer had been exhausted. We ripped through the barricade; a stinging cut in blue blood. We set ablaze the buildings, red weakness creeping up the steel ribs. We destroyed and hated, and we screamed. We metastasised, and we exulted in the sensation. The storm crackled above, the sky bruising ever deeper as the sun sought the refuge of night.

So we burned. Burned with passion, and hate, and wrath most of all. We flowed through the streets, a rumbling, ripping, tearing crowd, and it felt wonderful. To lose ourselves in the flame of our anger, to become an impulse, a synapse snapping into action. There was no more rot within our hearts eating us away, no more worry that tomorrow may steal our future. The rot had been burned away in our rage, our fever had cooked the virus from our system. We sought ever greater fury, as we tore and ruined.

Why were we here? The reason became clear to us. The buildings around us, the bones of the city, the streets below its blood, they were sick. The rot had found us from where it had festered deep in every basement, every office, and every corner. They needed to burn away, to have their immune systems drenched in boiling blood, and we were the fire. The night pulled on as the stars burned their own lives above.

We were together, united in wrathful oneness, fury our totality.

Then, the sun was rising again. I walked, feet sore on the cold tarmac and sky powder blue. Empty and alone, I was returned to myself. Rage had been my ablution, and – I hoped – my salvation.

Waking the Devil

Salvatore DiFalco

Some bastard was playing the bagpipes under my balcony first thing in the morning. All my grunts, gasps and growls could not penetrate that screechy wall of noise and reach the silly bugger. So what it came down to was myself going down to the street, spinning like a dervish, telling the kilted cretin that he had woken the wrong devil if that was his aim.

"Stop it!" I cried. "Stop it before I tear you to pieces!"

He spotted me and disengaged the slobbered blowpipe. The wheezing and screeching subsided and expired in a whiny diminuendo.

"Ay, laddie," he said, his tam o' shanter squint, kilt atilt, hairy arse exposed like a gnome needing a shave. "You don't like me playing?"

"Are you asking for a subjective aesthetic evaluation, or a general assessment?"

"You're gatherin' your brows like a gatherin' storm, sae help me god. Care, mad to see a beast sae unhappy."

The gibberish, the gibberish, always with the gibberish. People are fucked. Do they know they are fucked? Perhaps they do in some deep recess of their hollowness and insignificance. And I was accused of being primitive, of wallowing in my own primitivism. I never fully understood what that meant. But I'm certain it was pejorative. They mark you, then they tell you your services are no longer required. They ask nothing about your family, the little children, the little lady, working so hard to feed and keep them clean, and how you will finance all of that activity and growth. No, they ask nothing.

"Why, oh why," I said, "did you choose to strangle a banshee under my balcony this morning? How do you know I wasn't sleeping?"

"When Mungo's mither hang'd hersel'—a doublin' storm roared thro' the woods. I went thither and played me heart out bold like Johnny Barleycorn."

Oy, where was this guy taking me? The music was one thing, but the incomprehensible badinage rubbed vinegar in the wound. And yet, I felt no immediate need to violent the man. To violent him now, after we had established rapport, would be crude. Moreover, the idea of touching him repulsed me. My nostrils twitched. I smelled horse. I glanced down the cobblestone street and saw no horse or horse shit and heard no clop or whinny, and yet the unmistakable stench persisted and ripened with each moment. Scotty looked guilty as hell. The man either slept in a stable or dropped hygiene classes in prep school.

"Yo, Scotty, a little spritz of b.o. juice for the armpits after showering works for me. And you might wanna check out scented wipes for the nethers. My next door neighbour, a retired cartoonist who's lost his colon, swears by them."

The bagpipes sighed.

"The swats sae ream'd in Tammie's noddle."

"Don't smart mouth me, Scotty. Don't gibber away like that thinking because I don't know what the fuck you're saying I'm gonna let you off the hook. Yo, I'm not known for my forgiving ways. By the way, do know who I am? Do you know who I am, you fucking haggis-munching, horse-smelling tosser?"

He took offense to this and without relinquishing the bagpipes started circling me like a Highland warlock—raised hands and arched brows suggesting sinister magical powers or magical thinking at the very least. Who can keep a straight face with all this? He was going to turn me into a frog or something haha. Unless it was an unfamiliar bagpipe fighting style. I could see the chanter causing problems in a dust up. Something about the airbag also made me hungry, hard to explain. I had missed breakfast, but nothing about it looked appetizing.

"Wi' tippeny, we fear nae evil, we'll face the devil!"

"Don't fucking call me that, boy-o! That's copyrighted!"

"I'll coost your duddies to the wark!"

"Fuck was that? Coost my what? What did you just say?"

"Do cutty-sarks cleekit your mind?"

This was a slur. In any dialect this was a slur. Enough with this bozo, I thought. I started spinning. When I start spinning I create a powerful vortex. Ask anyone who knows me. The Scotsman went flying head over heels and any eyes that happened upon the tumble witnessed the saga of hirsute bollocks knocking like clackers as they rose with his thighs and bouncing like naked mice back to Earth. The bagpipes whined and it was this unmusical, dissonant whining that cinched it for me.

The Scotsman rose to his feet and straightened out his kilt. He picked up his fallen tam o' shanter and fitted it on his head. Blood trickled from his right ear, further blushing the ginger mutton chop framing that side of his face. The bagpipes remained shouldered despite the vortex, and he began to pump his arm as though he wanted to start up again. I was having none of it.

"Final warning," I said. "You play one more note on that thing and I will end you."

"To give music is me charge. I want to scre's the pipes and gart them skirl."

"But I cannot tolerate it! A violin, yes. An accordion, of course, or even a gentle hornpipe. Hoot hoot. How simple and nice. But not this, my man. Not this ungodly—"

"A tomahawk, wi blude red-rusted, are you, wi' a wee heart rotten, black as muck."

Fu-kit, I thought. I started spinning again, faster this time, faster. Things flew around, wrappers, twigs, dust and leaves. Buddy with the bagpipe and the speech impediment lost his bearings and wound up flopping into a polluted trough across the street where horses once drank before it killed them all. Finally, I saw the tam o' shanter soar above the vortex like some kind of strange plaid bird. It amused me.

Everyone is Broken

William Falo

The raccoon hissed at me. Someone caught him in a trap. It was meant to kill. Probably targeted raccoons. A throwaway animal. Disposable to some people. I know how he feels. I was like him. I was discarded. Forgotten about.

The wire was cutting into his fur. He snapped at me with a ferocity I could only imagine. I wore oven mitts to avoid the razor-sharp teeth, but that made me clumsy.

The raccoon managed to get off the table and started banging into the wall.

The door opened.

"Molly, do you need help?"

"Grab him."

We managed to get him on the table. I cut the wires off his paws and we got him in a carrier. The veterinarian would check him in the morning.

"Teamwork." Alex smiled. I didn't.

"Thanks." I walked out the door.

"Molly." He called out.

"Do you want to go somewhere?" I pretended not to hear him and got in my car. I prayed it would start. It did and I drove away without looking back.

I needed a second job. The money as an animal care assistant wasn't enough. The greyhound track ran night races and I got a job taking bets. Some guy on the streets got me the job when he went into rehab.

The greyhounds chased a rabbit around the track until they ran into a net. It was stupid. Dangerous. I heard stories that I didn't like. Broken legs, wounds, crippled dogs that were killed if they didn't win.

Nobody knew I worked there. Then I saw Alex looking at me. Sad eyes. He shook his head.

When I clocked out, he was standing by my car.

"How can you work here?"

"You followed me." The best defense is a good offense.

"Yes. I…"

I put my hand up. "You're a stalker."

He stepped back. "I did follow you, but look where you work."

"Damn it. Don't you think I hear the stories? I have a heart. I don't have nobody to help me. I need money to live. I was a missing child. Did you know that?" I clenched my fists. "I lived in the storage area of a decrepit wildlife park. I snuck in and helped the animals. One day, they put me in foster care. I lived with six families."

"I didn't know."

"Not one of them wanted to adopt me." I blew the black stringy hair out my eyes.

"I'm sorry."

"I only desired a family and I never got it."

I got in my car. I fumed and wished I could make someone feel my wrath. My chest hurt. Sometimes my heart skips a beat. A doctor told me to avoid anger. He said it was from years of starvation and other things. I held my chest and took deep breaths. It could be dangerous.

Alex stared at me. "Are you okay?"

I rolled the window down. "Go home. It's just a heart attack."

"What?"

"Just kidding." I started the car.

"Why do you care?"

"I don't know." He looked out at the track. "I lost a sister a few years ago."

"What happened?"

"Drunk driver." He wiped his eyes. "She was tough."

"Why follow me?"

"You remind me of her. You're so tough I like that. You're like the raccoon we helped today. Fierce."

"Maybe just broken."

"No. Everyone is broken. You're tough." I didn't feel tough.

The next day, I went back to the track. I started at the ticket window, but after the races I walked to the stables. A few dogs limped around. One of them was worse than the others. She held her leg up. A man came toward the dog.

I snapped pictures.

"What the hell are you doing?'

"I want that dog."

"She's badly injured. She's in pain."

"I'll help her."

"I can't do that."

"I'll report this place for animal cruelty and put it on the internet, plus I work here. Illegally. I can report that too."

He shook his head then pulled out some papers. "Her name is Fierce Freya." He wrote on some paper and gave it to me. My heart raced.

I carried her to my car. Maybe saving one dog is enough to make up for all the bad I'd done.

"You're the owner now?" Alex was by my car.

"Yes." I put my hand over my heart. "Why are you here? Are you stalking me again?'

"No. Are you okay?"

"I'll survive. Let's get her to the animal hospital."

Alex carried Fierce Freya into the animal hospital. My chest burned and I readied for another skip. It was a big one and blacked out.

*

The sound of someone snoring woke me up and I saw Alex on a chair.

"The dog?' I yelled out. Alex jumped up and hit the tray sending water across the floor.

"Molly. How do you feel?'

"Terrible. How is Fierce Freya?"

"She's going to be okay, but she needs surgery."

"I don't have the money to pay for that."

"I do. She will be our dog."

"I'm not able to care for anyone."

"The doctor said you will be okay if you take the meds."

"Oh, so you're my parent now." I laughed.

"No. A friend who cares."

He reached out and I let him hold my hand for a few minutes.

*

Now, I walk with a smile for a few minutes a day. It's a start. It's not as easy as I thought. There are many things that can make me sad and angry. Animal cruelty, bad drivers, lack of money, greed, lack of empathy, intolerance, abuse of all kinds.

My heart hasn't skipped a beat. I see Fierce Freya every day and Alex too. In that order, since Freya always greets me at his door. The track is still open. I am banned from entering it. I tried. Pressure is on them though and they take a little better care of the dogs, but it won't last. That's okay, because I won't give up either. Like Freya I am fierce.

New Delights Every Day

Jeffrey Weisman

A vision of wrath might see steam pouring out of flaring nostrils, an evil aura emanating from large red eyes, pointed sharpened nails at the end of long fingers.

But people don't use the term wrath much anymore: an old English term now replaced by anger or fury or rage or scorn. Television or movie monsters, vampires and zombies, or evil characters exhibit wrath. We mere mortals just exhibit extreme anger.

Look around in society. Casual anger can grow into wrath from the many absurd obnoxious affronts we face us each day.

Consider *obesity*. One-third of Americans are fat. We're not talking chubby here. We're talking fat. And why should this cause anger, you ask?

Lack of self-control, beyond any genetic factors, leads to porcine practices. And that fat leads to diabetes. More and more people contract diabetes every day. Our healthcare costs rise. Fat people make me spend more money for my healthcare insurance. You can bet I'm angry.

On an airplane, have you ever sat next to a large person? Their waist and body extend over the arm rest onto you.

Asking the cabin attendant to move your seat often results in a seat next to another large person. The odds are one in three.

Tax cuts for the rich make me angry. The swells in power take care of their rich buddies. The poor people, the middle class, get next to nothing. And the bastards lie when they say the tax cut will benefit all.

Bollocks. The cuts benefit the rich. The alleged "trickle down" theory has proved not to work. They lied about it when Reagan was president. They still do. The powers of industry reinvest in their companies and give nothing back to the workers.

Those $1,000 gifts last year made them one-time heroes. Note that they won't repeat this largesse. The owners just take their tax cut money and place it in their own accounts.

Politics – I'm right, you're wrong – incurs anger. Endless emails come from people favoring their party. They won in 2016. Yet they continue to send emails and other messages. Insecurity? Somehow they think that a barrage of messages will convince me. Please, save your media money.

Speaking of *political media*, have you seen the extent of lies in advertising? No one talks about issues, positions, accomplishments. They just tear down the opposition. They find facts and distort them.

"So-and-so pays taxes late." The law allows late tax paying. But the opponent makes this into a crime. And the gullible public believes the innuendo.

"So-and-so misses committee meetings." But the lying commercial doesn't tell you the opponent isn't on that committee and not expected to attend. Pure lies and a deluded public.

Millions of dollars across the country are wasted this way. Awful.

Voter ID laws perpetuate Jim Crow practices. The Supreme Court cancelled the Voting Rights Act. Simultaneously, conservative states enacted voter suppression laws mainly against minorities to register and vote.

Same-day registration and voting eliminated. Picture IDs, not needed for years, become the new norm. Reduced early voting days and no Sunday voting. IDs requiring addresses. (Native American citizens living on reservations don't have addresses. Pure voter suppression.)

The suppression goes further. If an election official misspelled or wrote the person's name incorrectly – through no fault of the voter – that person couldn't vote. The disqualified victims were usually black or Latino or Native American. Racism still rules.

Men who do not flush urinals also contribute to my wrath. Do these people think someone will murder them and the police will want chemical evidence of their life? Do they do this at home? Maybe their spouse flushes for them. How quaint.

Drivers not turning on their headlights in rain bothers me as well. Cars without lights make them difficult to see, a danger to all. Sometimes I want to ram them with my car.

Whew! Taken together this litany of anger-producers causes my wrath to explode. I must cool down. Thanks for listening.

Natural Born Killer

Jim Bell

The encounter is violent, merciless. Her prey tries to escape, but there is little hope. She is born for this pursuit. Skills passed down through her ancestors, centuries of survival in the wild, encourage brutal instincts to take hold. Kill or be killed. Ruthlessness is rewarded. She is a beast of nature. Rage is unleashed in a torrent of fury. Her victim will suffer the wrath of her primal needs.

She is a husky, a breed of dog that shares the DNA of the wild grey wolf. Her ancestors were bred nearly 3,000 years ago by the Chucki people of northeastern Asia to survive in the wild. She is tireless in the hunt. Evolution has given her the strength to cover great distances while expending a minimum amount of energy. Speed and endurance are part of her heritage.

Strong, muscular shoulders allow her to overpower and pull down prey with ease. Her medium-sized build, at fifty-five pounds, is ideal for endurance. If she were larger, her heart would struggle to sustain pumping blood and oxygen to her extremities. Her large lung capacity enables her to cover miles of ground without tiring.

As she runs, an innate drive to conquer kicks in. All is natural, fluid movement. Her long strides reduce the gap between predator and prey in seconds. She has a single focus: capture her victim. She closes in. The grace and beauty of her motions in the chase transform into a scene of unrelenting power and savagery in the conquest.

Jaws open, then quickly seize her prey in a vice-like grip. A high-pitched squeal, evidence of the agony her victim is suffering, pierces the air. She senses the animal's struggle to escape and violently jerks her head from side to side, rendering her victim senseless. With one quick motion, she releases her hold, only to reset her teeth deep into her victim's back. Again and again, she strikes and rips flesh from the prey.

The lifeless body hangs limp in her jaws. She carries the kill to her bed as large balls of stuffing trail behind her.

"Oh, Panda!" her master cries out, viewing the torn carcass strewn about the living room. "That's the third squeak toy you've destroyed this week."

Circular Quay

Andrew Grenfell

She reaches the designated meeting point as the late afternoon sun shatters the harbour into thousands of knives of light. There is nowhere to sit.

A red electric scooter glides past. They have been turning up everywhere lately. Apparently you just find one, using the App, picking it up from wherever the previous rider left it, and away you go. You have to have the App.

They had hurriedly agreed to meet here, at the wrong end of Circular Quay. Though now that she thinks about it, it was really his suggestion. What is there to do here? Nowhere to eat but overpriced tourist traps, an over-peopled strip sandwiched between the relentless concrete of the city jungle and the dogged sloshing of the harbour. At the opposite end of the CBD from his apartment, where they usually rendezvous'ed. A hotel or two, the squat white of the Opera House like a squashed butterfly. And everywhere tourists with their over-bright clothes, their bare legs, their bumbags and cameras.

Then she realises why. Of course. The perfect place to break it up.

She feels a heat in her cheeks, on the backs of her legs, in her chest.

When her mother was taken into hospital, where was he? *Babe, I can't, I've got to work late.* The only time he'd used the word *Babe*. Like she was an infant.

She really is working herself into a tizz. Her phone is nearly out of battery, otherwise she might distract herself from her burning thoughts with it. Instead her butt is becoming numb from sitting on concrete edging. She stands up and paces. Without sunglasses – a forgotten victim of the mad rush to get herself out of the house and to work this morning – the shards of light slamming off the water pierce straight into her head.

She contemplates the water for a moment. She pulls her blouse away from her sticky skin and then surreptitiously adjusts her bra.

She composes an email to her boss in her head and imagines with some satisfaction the Send button exploding into pixellated confetti from the force of her mouse click when she presses it.

She watches the ferries slip in and out of their slots at the quay, sleekly green, symphonic in their own way.

In the early days they had been a proper couple, turning heads, *perfect for each other* said her friends, then it had devolved into what? A glass of wine or two, forced laughter, a sardonic kind of affection, regular sex. Things starting to be taken for granted. *Him* taking *her* for granted.

Another scooter passes, so close she feels the wind of its passing. Its rider smugly upright, unbeholden to the pushing slog of muscle otherwise required to perambulate. You pick up the scooter and ride, escaping yourself. Acquire, discard, repeat.

How he said her tossing her long black hair like that while she was on top of him drove him completely wild. She has the urge to crop it short, maybe in the style of that woman over there, something like Anne Hathaway in her pixie phase, perhaps. See what he'd say then.

It's not like there aren't any other men in this world. Take that bloke over there, wearing a suit the exact same navy colour as hers, frowning as he looks up from his phone. Would he blow her off on the weekend on a whim to spend time with his rugby mates? Tell her at great length about his crappy work day but show no interest in hers?

She feels it in her gut, a wrenching anger at being kept waiting, at being the one jilted, at wasting her time with him, and further down, deep in the pit of her stomach, a black helplessness in the face of her mother's likely passing. *No more than a month*, the doctors had said.

Howard. What kind of a name is that, anyway? She hates the softness of it, the wide vowelness in it, like an abyss.

Pickup, ride, discard, repeat.

There he is at last, harried through a new tide of tourists spilling out of the hotel, his battered leather briefcase nearly twisting out of his grip, a dumb grin taking over his features as he spots her through the throng. Thinking he's the one in control, that he can dictate how it will go from here, can force her into victimhood.

Well, it won't be her this time. Not this time.

Not this time.

Hell Hath No Fury Like the Hangry

Jo Hocking

I enter hell with my handbasket – Woolworths at lunchtime on a Saturday. No pentagrams on the floor – just decals advertising two-for-one specials on Hass avocadoes. There's a devilish thrill in attempting this risky quest without my glucose tablets. I should get out of here alive, but there's no escaping the DEFCON 5 disaster about to hit the store.

12:30. Four hours since I've eaten. The first signs manifest – elevated tell-tale heart-rate, ghost skull rodents gnaw at my eye sockets, the bakery zooms into Google Maps-like focus as if I've drained the BWS' nastiest goon sack. Lights, music, people – everything is escalating from minor annoyance to cataclysmic trigger.

My mission – pick up dinner ingredients before I strike down upon all with great vengeance and furious hanger. My strategy – move swiftly and take no prisoners. My enemy – blood sugar dropping faster than the going rate paid to farmers for fresh produce.

Trying desperately to flee a rapidly descending cloud of brain fog, I bolt for the meat freezer. Chicken. I eat chicken, me. Yes. A teenage Woolies worker, burdened with a massive trolley and an inability to move beyond a snail's pace, scribbles

20c discounts off honey soy chicken kebabs with her Sharpie. A pack of twelve poultry-loving scabs attacks, blocking my path.

Sugarless blood pounds my cranium – the dreaded hangry head! Tolerance and civility evaporate. Move or incur my wrath! Elbows up and eyes narrowed, I launch myself into the scrum. A middle-aged woman shakes her head disapprovingly, a hipster drops her probiotics, a nana boasting an impressive chin of stubble breathes "Madre de Dios" at my audacity. I bust through the pack but can't process the choices in the overwhelming chicken cornucopia. Concerned by the brutal death stares and possible presence of damning CCTV, I grab something pink and flee for the nearest aisle.

Bad idea. The world sharply lurches to the right. Desperately grabbing the nearest shelf for purchase against the rolling tide of vertigo, I press my face against this week's cereal specials. Letters blur – I'm beyond reading but brand recognition takes over. A wave of completely unjustified rage. Why don't they call it Nutri Gain since all the sugar just makes you fat? Why must Quaker Oats literally ram religion down my throat? Why doesn't Uncle Tobys have an apostrophe? I feel like snap, crackle and popping somebody in the face.

International foods aisle – I can grab something – anything. The multicultural palette of colours – orange butter chicken, green Thai curry, Mongolian black bean – frustrates and confuses me. A pink-haired twenty-something wearing yoga pants, a hoodie emblazoned with 'Dream, Believe, Succeed' and a cloak of self-absorption pushes a fully loaded trolley while texting. A combination of such reckless endanger-ment and pigeon-toed wheels cause the trolley to veer to the right, clipping the top layer of skin from my ankle. I howl in pain and then wince at the ice-pick the sound drives into my skull.

"Watch what you're doing, you stupid scrag!" I bark at her, impressed at my ability to get the words out in the correct order.

Then I notice the white headphones. She removes one. "Did you say something?" I briefly consider glassing her with a jar of KanTong Sweet and Sour, but stride off down the aisle in a huff and grab the brightest thing I can see which is a canary yellow Mexican fajita kit. Mission accomplished.

Queues, queues, everywhere. I dismiss the ethical option to wait in line to keep pimply-faced kids in jobs. This is a full-blown sugar crisis. It's Lord of the Flies. My brain trails off into the dazed mists as I think of Lord of the Fries. Mmm … loaded chips … My feet keep moving and I realise that I've wandered off in a cloud of confusion.

Snap back to reality. Somehow I'm in the confectionery aisle. It's a real-life wonky Willy Wonka boat scene in chunderous spinning technicolour. A kaleidoscope of Cadbury purple blurs with the hazy hazelnut of Snickers and melts into gooey caramel Lindt balls. Packets of party mix bob up and down, Allen's snakes sinuously slither, boxes of M&Ms rattle, tubes of Chupa Chups float like bright bubbles. Colours surge in a churning, boiling, heaving, seething sea of saccharine.

Then I spot the lighthouse offering sanctuary from the storm. Promising the purest hit and the swiftest end to the swirling mental hell of the hangry head.

I snatch the orange packet of Wizz Fizz Original Sherbet from the shelf and rip it open with my shaky hands. The sachets tumble out. I drop to my knees, shamelessly grabbing at the precious stash like a frenzied animal. I tear the first sachet open with my teeth and shoot the contents straight down the back of my throat. Stuff you, useless plastic spoon! Half misses my mouth, lightly dusting my top, neck and chin. A second sachet, a third, a fourth, five or six to be sure. One packet left –

might as well finish the last few white lines. It's a jolt of calorific crack to the hippocampus.

Rage dissipating … Fuzziness clearing … Humanity returning …

With a layer of fine, white powder covering the floor, the confectionery aisle resembles a scene from Narcos. So, it's not surprising to see the equivalent of the DEA – Woolworths security. I also note the prickly faced nana slinking off into the background with three packets of discount kebabs and a knowing smirk. I hope she slips on a grape on the way out.

I'm caught white-mouthed and red handed, sprawled in the evidence of my crime. With no option for plausible denial, I look the beefy security guard right in the eye and hold out my wrists. "Guilty as charged. Where do I sign up for hanger management?"

Puissant

Peter Lingard

You wanna know if I was taking a piss? Yeah, I was, but it wasn't *the* piss, if ya know what I mean. I got caught short after downing a few brews. Now, because some arsehole made a video, I'm subject to anger and ridicule everybleedinwhere. And, let's face it; the arsehole kept his finger on the button because he figured there was money in it. That, or he thought his fifteen minutes had arrived. There were three other guys and we were pissing in unison. Four guys voiding their bladders and making steam. Effing cameraman didn't even notice the beauty of four bonded blokes pissing together. The little shit must've scurried to a spot where he could make me the star of the show. How come he left ma mates in the background? Don't they deserve equal billing? Jack's a successful builder, Dave an architect and Shane's some kind of expert with computers. I'm just a dumb footballer.

So now everyone in Melbourne has seen me hosing down a wall of the St Kilda cop shop. Shit! Ten to one I'm on Facebook. By the way, we're playin' The Saints on Sunday, so I should get a bonus.

I don't know why suburbanites get their knickers in a twist over me drainin' off. If the Cecil B. DeMille wannabee hadn't been around, nobody'd know about it. It'd be like that tree falling in the forest. I hose down the wall of a cop shop when there're no cops around (not to mention security cameras) and this nerd from East Podunk captures the scene on his rinky-dink mobile. I suppose I shouldn't say East Podunk ... there might be such a place and its citizens could be real nice people. Unlike the amateur movie producer who actually lives in Mount Waverley. Not to put Mount Waverley down either; I'm sure they never invited the snake ta make his nest there. I'll be visiting him after I've finished tellin' you about the shit I'm in. He'll being feelin' my wrath, I can tell you!

I was surprised ta find out he dated my sister. I fail to see how that can be a coincidence. He must've been stalkin' me, waitin' for his opportunity. I'll have to ask him 'bout that. He'll give it up soon enough. I considered signing my autograph on his chest with a six-inch nail, seeing as how he's such a fan, but it'd mark me as well as 'im. I'll try to restrain myself from layin' a finger on 'im, but I will scare the shit out of 'im.

He's from the Northern Territory so I've no idea how him an' Sheila met. Maybe she sold herself as a mail-order bride ... or is it male-order bride? She's like that, anything to be different. She tried being a lesbian once but, while she liked the eternally erect accessories, she didn't think much of rollin' around with another woman. I haven't spoken to her since the so-called incident. I wonder if she knows the whole story of her brother's embarrassment at the hands of her paparazzi-like lover. He surely wouldn't 'ave the balls to tell 'er. Maybe I'll drop-kick the son-of-a-bitch back to Darwin for her. That'd add a new meaning to 'photo-finish'.

Being physical with people is what brings me half-a-mill a season. So, to the *Herald Sun* and all the blue-hairs in suburbia, I announce my intention to remain the same. I've got so many clauses in ma contract, if I became the all-Australian clean-cut hero, I could end up paying the suits that employ me. If they suspend me for a game or two, it'll just be more time for ma body ta recover from the last beatin' it took on the field. Given the way the club expects me ta play, I still get cash stuffed in ma boots when suspended.

That bookies' clerk's story last year made me money, too. I'll bet on almost anythin' and if I wasn't such a winner, nobody'd care. I make a very nice supplemental income (my accountant's words) out of gamblin' on cricket, rugby, soccer and, yeah, footy. But I never bet on me own team or the team we're up against. The AFL fined me and promised they'd ensure players kept the integrity of the game sacrosanct. Sacrosanct this! They should come down the pub where some of us meet every Thursday and, over a few wet ones, decide what injury information and other team-changing news we'll sell ta the bookies.

When all the do-gooders have done criticizing me for ma sins, they still want me ta be a thug on the field. I'm one of the guys they can brag about to the Yanks. *See this guy play. He doesn't need a helmet or pads.* The so-called ardent fans wear their scarves, wave their banners and wet themselves when we score. They hurl abuse at us, drink their brews, and stuff their faces while we sweat and bleed. Listen to their bloodthirsty roar when I drop-kick some kid who's just startin' out. Then, when the pompous bastards get home and sober up, they think they have the right to expect me ta be different off the field.

D'ya ever notice how incidents that get a man put on report are played over and over on television? The suburban couch-potatoes love ta see the violence from a safe distance. I've got news for all those who expect me to act like a so-called gentleman away from the stadium: Australian Rules Football is not a gentleman's game. I don't have a lot of talent, hell, the game doesn't call for a lot of talent. I earn my half-mill by being a hard-nosed son-of-a-bitch with speed and stamina. I don't have a game-face. It's me out there.

Being what those suburbanites call normal would be costly. I'll make sure the effin' moviemaker understands that.

Sub

Elaine Barnard

It was 5 A.M. when they called. As usual I went into panic mode scurrying back and forth in the bedroom to get my head straight. I needed to exercise, make breakfast, dress conservatively, gas the car and get to Capo High by 7 A.M. Today's assignment was drama substitute. I prayed he'd left plans; any plans would smooth the day. My son was up but still in his pajamas imitating me in panic mode. "Hey," I said, "Knock it off and get dressed or we'll both be late."

An hour later we were in the car. Ryan was attempting to clean the windshield while I gassed up. I had to love him for making the effort. I dropped him at the Middle School. He disappeared before I could embarrass him with a hug.

Capo High emerged from the beach mist. It was an old school, stucco and red tile roof, imitating old Mexico in Southern California. A dry cactus garden surrounded it. Not a flower in sight. I put a newspaper over my head to keep my hair dry. If I got it wet it hung limp like spaghetti.

I checked in with Eloise. She seemed snappish this morning like she'd stayed up late watching TV. I never had that luxury since I started subbing hoping to eventually get a full-time position.

"Did Mister Cohen leave plans?" I asked smelling the remains of Eloise's breakfast in the trash.

"Does he ever?" She slammed her stapler on a stack of papers for emphasis. "His classroom's down the hall. Take a right. First door on the left. The kids are already in there. You're late."

I took that right down the dim hallway with the paint peeling in yellowish globs, and took a deep breath before I entered. Forty smirking kids waited. Then I saw the water pail strung up over the door. But their trick was a failure. I closed the door carefully and approached the monsters. "Whose idea was this?"

Not a peep. Instead the head clown, spooning an avocado, started passing it around the room. Everyone was slurping avocado. No one was listening as I pleaded with them to open their Shakespeare to *Richard the Third*, thinking his evil machinations would be appropriate. Groans and more groans as brownies were passed, crumbs littering the floor. "Okay," I said to the kid who'd passed the avocado and was now feeding dried mango to his girlfriend. "You!"

"Me?"

"Yes, you. Get up here and teach the class."

He strutted to the front, a grin pasting his face. I sat down in his seat and slurped avocado, chewed mango, put my feet on his desk, turned to the other kids and yawned. His face grew red. He stood immobilized. The class was silent, waiting for what would happen next.

"Now," I instructed, "step into the hallway and return through that door."

Some Gods Deserve to Die

Cormac Stagg

I felt my old heart quiver and I hung my head to cry when I heard a former Anglo high priest say, "Some gods deserve to die."

The god of men in marching boots who kill and maim and loot, I must now make it clear to you is just not worth a hoot.

Some gods deserve to die I say, when hooded hoodlums are still free, to raise their burning crosses in the land of liberty.

And the gods of literalism of strictly black and white, who simply can't abide the shades of gray that ushers in the light.

Again I say make no mistake: some gods deserve to die. The gods who say that gays and queers and dykes and transvestites, are all banned and damned for sure. At least until the happy day they take the holy cure.

And while we're in this space we should also face that the two-trick pony god has surely run his race. Because he only seems to care that the righteous ones get rich. And that those lucky righteous few reserve their hateful scorn for the poor and wretched aborting girl whose child is never born.

Some gods deserve to die I say, in one more heartfelt grip. Like the all-exclusive hierarchal patriarchal god, who puts the lads in charge then pops down from the heavens, once or twice I guess, to clean up their highfaluting and unholy bloody mess.

And who seems to have this habit of convincing religionists of every type and stripe, to forget the rest, you found the best, the tested and true. But mind yourselves and don't forget to keep the holy rules, or we might just have to cast you back into the sinners' brew.

But there is a god who with the rest and perhaps even more than most, well and truly does deserve a fiery funeral roast. He is the all-consuming pernicious god of wrath and fear, who lurks about in our poor hearts and dampens down our cheer.

He is the undisputed reigning champion god of fire and brimstone rant. About the hellfires waiting for sinners far and wide, unless they do their penance and get god back on side.

Yes he knows his stuff this mythic god of wrath and grim, and he wields his whip to make of us a pure and spotless sign. And prepared for the great muster where unless we've toed his line, then things for us might not ever, ever turn out to fine.

But I say to you in earnest don't be fooled by his fat lie, for he really is just another god who now deserves to die.

I felt my old heart quiver and I hung my head to cry when I heard a former Anglo high priest say – "Some gods deserve to die".

Vengeance

Kate Mahony

At Brisbane their flight to New Zealand was delayed. Ignoring the faint protests of his wife, Kent complained loudly to the person at the airline desk and was eventually handed two $20 food vouchers.

Their café bill came to $38. The young cashier said he couldn't give change. Kent gave him the full benefit of his most wrathful stare but the teenager wouldn't budge.

Kent scowled and grabbed a banana from the counter instead.

He sat down to eat his soup and sandwich at a table and began boasting to a nearby group of fellow passengers about his success at scoring a food voucher from the airline desk. None of them had thought to do so which rather pleased Kent.

A short time later, his wife came back to say that their flight was being called early. Thrusting his scattered belongings into his duffle bag, he slung it over his shoulder and stormed off leaving her to follow with a heavy-laden cabin bag. His wife seemed about to call after him but he was too far ahead.

Three and a half hours later they arrived at Auckland International Airport. Kent strode through the Nothing To Declare lane well ahead of his wife. A small sniffer dog on a lead approached him and became agitated. It leapt up and began to paw at his duffle bag. Alerted to a prohibited food item forbidden under New Zealand's strict bio-security laws, an official took a look inside. Something limp and yellow was found in the bottom of the bag.

As Kent paid the $400 fine for attempting to bring a banana into the country, his wife now several paces ahead turned back and pointed at him. She began to laugh. Quietly.

Even so, it was loud enough for her fellow passengers to hear as they passed by.

Stew

Paul Beckman

Jack's in his room, lying face down on his bed, propped up on his elbows reading a book, the autumn air blowing in from the open window next to the bed smells good. Without knocking, his father walks in about ten seconds behind his beer and cigar breath.

Jack watches his father move his hands to his belt.

Expecting another beating, but not knowing the reason, Jack crawls over to the window and climbs out and onto the garage roof. His father's too fat to get through the window, but he closes and locks it. He doesn't see Jack grab the gutter and then the downspout and slide down to the ground.

Jack's father yells to his wife, Sheila, to get a move on, he's ready for dinner.

Meekly she tells him, It'll be ready by the time he washes up.

The man of the house walks into the kitchen and glares at his wife and asks her who the hell she thinks he is that she has to tell him to wash up.

She tells him she was just timing how long it would take to set his place and bring the food to the table.

Snarling, he tells her that she has an answer for everything.

She dishes his food into a bowl and puts it in front of him telling him to eat his nice bowl of stew. His wife says she'll get the bread out of the oven and slice it up.

Not satisfied with his wife's subservience, he tells her that she knows he hates waiting when he's hungry.

She calls him honey and tells him to start on the stew.

Still with his hostile tone he complains that the kid's on the roof again and she has to do something about him.

She tells him she didn't send him there.

Not willing to give up his superiority, Jack's father tells his wife she didn't stop him either and then snarls for her to give him more stew and another beer.

Somehow the wife gets the courage up to offer him more stew but tells him no more beer.

Angry as all get-out he tells her that she's not his keeper and to get him that beer. Then he wants to know why his shoes weren't shined this morning for work.

Disgusted, she tells him he works construction and she cleaned the mud off. Pushing it, she asks if he wanted her to shine over the mud.

He dumps the pot of stew on the table and tells her shine this. Then he catches a movement at the kitchen door window.

Jack walks in and stands, arms folded like his father would do, and asks him why he thought it was okay to do what he just did. He tells his father he and his mother haven't eaten and he's got to clean up his mess.

Jack's father strains to stand, belches, takes a bottle-finishing swig of the beer and tells Jack that he can clean it up because that's all he's good for.

The mother runs over with a large spoon, rights the stew pot and begins to scoop the stew back in. The son walks to the corner, grabs a broom and dustpan, throws it at his father and tells him to clean up the floor.

The father reaches for his belt buckle and Jack, determined he won't take another beating, grabs the beer bottle by the neck and tells him to not even think about using the belt on him.

It wasn't for you, the father says, and his wife stops what she's doing and runs out the back door determined to not tolerate her husband's abuse again.

Her drunken husband yells after her that she's going to pay good for leaving the mess. Brandishing the beer bottle, the son threatens his father.

Jack's father, still holding the broom, jabs his son in the gut doubling him over. He slaps him with a meaty hand on his way down and tells Jack that now's as good a time as any for him to learn a lesson.

The sound of a clearing throat has them both turn towards the living room where the door is open and the bully's wife is standing, dripping tears, holding her husband's shotgun and he laughs at her. Taking the safety off she keeps it pointed at him. With quavering voice Jack's mother tells her husband to pack. He laughs and the mother pulls the trigger and blows a hole in the wall next to him. Pack, she tells him again and her husband realizes his wife isn't fooling around.

Personal Column

Grahame Maclean

The train heaved out of the station, leaving a grey smear of uncertainty across a fine rain.

He'd been lucky. The train had arrived as he walked onto the platform and he'd managed to get a seat by the window. The hard, slatted benches, fanning out from the carriage sides like old yellow teeth, were uncomfortable. The wood had cracked and sagged over the years of backsides and motion. The raw, splintered edges along the front of the bench dug into his legs with every jolt of the rails. But this was going to be a long journey, and any seat was better than sitting on the floor or standing in the corridors.

It was still dark as he looked out at the station. Rain tears streaked the smoke dirt windows. Rivulets danced across the glass in the jaded morning wind, illuminated by the fading glare of a solitary sodium light.

The ticket office had closed over a year ago, and the weeds grew where the queues once waited in line each morning. Train travel was free now to many. But that did little to raise the spirits as the train rolled onward towards an easterly dawn.

He took out a book, hoping to be able to read. The overhead lights—shuttered by the filth of age, or not working at all—gave little illumination. But they did something else. They turned the windows into mirrors. As he watched the sea of faces from the safety of anonymity, and the muted countryside slid past like a backdrop to a silent movie—and as the actors played their parts, and the rhythm of the rails built the tension in the sound track as the train picked up speed, he knew he was watching a film.

And then he saw the star.

She was sitting on the opposite side of the carriage in the row behind. By leaning forward, he could find the right angle and see her clearly. She looked very small, a waif with dark hair and large brown eyes. She wore a faded yellow cap, with a tiny rose print on the front, and a grey winter coat.

She seemed to be looking straight at him. But mirrors and imagination often play tricks. Of one thing he was certain. She was the most beautiful girl he'd ever seen, and this was far beyond physical attraction. She shone an inner light and honesty that he'd never seen before. He felt as though she had opened a door to his heart and walked right in. No warning. No knock. No . . . may I come in? This was like something he'd read about—and thought didn't exist. "Everyone has a soul mate," his mother used to say. "And not everyone ever finds them in this lifetime. But if you do . . . never let her go."

His mother's words rang round his head and he felt lost as he watched the film unfold . . . around his star.

Then she smiled.

"She's not smiling at me. It's a trick of the light," he whispered to himself. "But if I were living at home, I'd put a message in the personal column of the local paper. I'd say, 'I'm trying to contact the girl in the yellow cap with the rose on the front, who was on the early morning train—and now owns my heart . . . forever.'"

But he doubted she'd even noticed him.

*

Anna Braun lay with the others in the blackened remains of a wasted barn. The ragamuffin crowd of fearless souls who'd fought together as heroes were beginning to stir. She could hear noise. A whispered urgent chatter, barely audible, drifted breath to breath. There was a shout from somewhere down the lane. The entire crowd moved as one and stood looking into nothing. Someone pulled her to her feet as another shout split the air. It was time to leave. She took out her cap, pulled it on her head, and waited.

The driver loomed out of the still black morning.

"Come on you stinking bastards, move," he shouted. "I'll wait for five minutes, and if you're not on, you'll stay—and die." He spat in the dirt.

He was a foreigner. One of hundreds commandeered to start moving this exodus of human flesh to a new life. To him compassion was a weakness, and to cross him would incur wrath of such savagery that silence, and eyes fixed to the dirt road, were the only chance of survival.

"Come on," he said, "let's go."

They stumbled down the lane between the dark dripping hedgerows, and on to the field. The lorry was parked by the gate, the loading ramp down, and the engine still running.

"You've got two minutes," he said, and walked to his cab.

They scrambled inside onto a rusty floor, and as the last ones were dragged in, the driver set off. The journey was almost unbearable. The truck rattled along the rutted tracks on steel rims for three hours and arrived at the station as the train was about to leave. Anna ran with the crowd along the platform and someone pushed her through an open carriage door.

"Sit here," shouted a woman on one of the rear benches. She held out her hand and dragged Anna beside her. "We can all sit closer, there's plenty of room."

"Thank you very much," whispered Anna, as the final whistle shrieked.

The sour smell of thread-worn clothes and old sweat crept through the carriage like a shroud. Everyone huddled together and spoke in lighthearted whispers. But the voices of hope carried an edge of uncertainty and fear.

Yet something made Anna smile. She had no idea why. There was nothing here to be happy about. She lifted her head and stared towards the window. The train rushed on through a broken countryside, towards a grey colorless dawn . . . and she smiled again.

And even though she was blind, she had the strangest feeling that her eyes had found home.

The Two Marys

Gloria Garfunkel

I thought she was my best friend. "Sisters" we would say. It was like I was blind. No, deaf even. Like I was hearing the opposite of what she was saying. Like I would often laugh and feel embarrassed at the same time when she poked fun at me. But most of the time it seemed we laughed together. Told funny stories. Confided our insecurities. Only she was also filled with wrath, not towards me but the people she worked with. She felt they didn't give her enough respect. She decided to tell people she was a psychologist instead of a social worker. She felt that would get her the respect she sought. I was a psychologist. She asked if I thought it was ethical for her to call herself one publicly. That's what she had started telling people. I thought it unethical but stayed silent. She had already clearly made her decision.

I was married with children, and she was divorced three times with none. Actually, she told people she was a widow, as her last husband was dying in the hospital which held up the filing of the divorce papers which thus never went through. She would tell people her husband had died, which earned her sympathy. Also, it allowed her to keep control of the fortune her husband had made on his new mathematical models. It allowed her to tell his second wife and two daughters to get out of the house she had been in the midst of selling when he got sick, even though she and her husband had already moved to a condo in town. And then, when he died, she begged me to speak for her at his memorial service because no one else would represent her. Everyone he knew hated her. So I stood at the podium for my friend to say what a wonderful couple they were and how kind they both were to my children.

Many years later, while my children were young adults, my own husband died. I fell apart and my younger son took over, sending messages to all of our friends about the dates of the funeral and a month later, the memorial service. I was in a numb daze. I could barely speak. I couldn't cry at all, not even to this day, three years later. I am frozen. My life has stopped.

She didn't come to the funeral and didn't contact me. Before the memorial service, she claimed to have the flu. I didn't know people got the flu in August.

And slowly the truth came out, or actually several versions of it. She didn't attend the funeral because my son had sent the message to an out-of-date email and by the time she found it, it was too late. Later she admitted to not attending because she was insulted that the note was sent by him and not personally by me, the paralyzed one.

Meanwhile, another friend with the same name came up to me at the memorial service with her husband and complained that my older son wasn't speaking to her at all. She thought it was insulting and bizarre that he wasn't welcoming her to his father's memorial service. I assumed he was paralyzed and in a daze like me. I had no response. I didn't keep track of him at the service. I just focused on my potato salad. She was shaming me and I couldn't see it, telling me there was something wrong with my son and it was my fault.

Just like I couldn't see the shaming when my "sister" talked about going to a country club with her new Match.com boyfriend and laughed to my younger son and his girlfriend,

"Can you imagine your mother at a country club. Ha, ha, ha, ha!"

Status was important to both Marys. I often thought the only reason the first Mary liked me was because I went to Harvard. And her new country club boyfriend had gone to Yale. She ended up marrying him, after she stopped visiting me and cut me off. She had a long engagement and married him in Cambridge, England. I was not invited as we were no longer speaking. The second Mary cut me off as a friend because she only wanted friends who were writers with status and I was only a writer.

I think about each occasionally. I think about the first Mary lying to me about the funeral and the memorial service, what a good friend I had been at her husband's memorial service, and what a terrible friend she was to me. I think about the second Mary writing to me that she would make a New Year's resolution to contact me. She never did.

Somewhere inside of me sat shame, grief, anxiety, and wrath, but I couldn't feel them. Just like I couldn't feel anything. Just like I still can't feel anything. Except the potato salad I buy at Whole Foods.

Dora the Mouse Slayer

Steve Carr

Dora shook the dustpan in front of Albert's nose. The dead
mouse bounced up and down in the dustpan. "That is a mouse.
You're supposed to kill them, or at least want to," Dora said to
Albert.

He sniffed it, and then turned his head and sauntered off.

"Useless cat," Dora grumbled. "It's because of the mice that
get into this house that I got you from the shelter to begin with."

She picked the broom up from the floor and carried it and
the dustpan to the back screen door, pushed it open, and
pitched the mouse into the moonlit backyard. She closed the
door and placed the broom against the wall and the dustpan on
the floor beside it. She washed her hands in the kitchen sink,
poured a cup of coffee, and then sat down at the table. Just as
she was about to take a sip from the cup, a movement along the
base of the stove caught her eye. With the steam from the
coffee heating her face, she peered over the cup's rim. Then she
saw it. A small mouse scurried from beneath the stove, across
the floor, and behind the curtain that hung from the sink,
hiding the pipes.

"Albert!" she screamed out. "There's another one." She
put the cup down, stood up from the table and grabbed the
broom. Grasping the handle with both hands she stood in front
of the sink and raised the broom above her head. "A widow

who needs her sleep shouldn't have to chase mice in the middle of the night," she mumbled.

Albert slowly walked into the kitchen, stopped to clean his whiskers, and then strolled over to Dora and rubbed his fat body against her legs.

"Albert, there's a mouse under the sink," Dora snapped. "You remember me mentioning those, don't you? They're those filthy little rodents who multiply like cockroaches. For my seventy-first birthday one of them crapped right on my last piece of birthday cake. You heard me right, Albert. It left me a mouse turd for my birthday. Now act like a cat and go under the sink and chase out the mouse and I'll smash it with the broom."

Using her slippered foot she pushed Albert under the curtain. A moment later the cat stuck its head out and softly meowed. Resignedly, Dora lowered the broom, returned to her chair, and leaned the broom against the table. "You lack killer instinct," she said to Albert, as he stepped out from under the sink and sat at her feet. "Some things just have to be killed, and mice are one of those things." She took a long sip of coffee and then looked down at Albert who was licking his butt. "As I always said to my dear, departed Albert, 'Wrath is an ugly thing, except for when it's taken out on a mouse'."

The cat strolled through the kitchen and disappeared into the living room.

Dora finished the coffee and was just about to stand up when the mouse ran out from under the sink and dashed across the kitchen floor. Dora hastily grabbed the broom as she quickly stood, and stepping onto a small throw rug, her fluffy blue slipper caught on the rug, propelling her onto the floor. At that moment she saw the mouse run into the living room. She lay there for a moment with pain shooting up her leg from her throbbing ankle. She slowly crawled up, leaving the slipper in the rug, and hopped into the living room on one foot, dragging the broom behind her.

Albert was curled up on a pillow on the sofa.

"Where did the mouse go, you good-for-nothing cat?"

Albert ran his paw over his face and gazed sweetly at Dora.

Balanced on one foot, Dora raised the broom to her shoulder, holding it like a soldier with a rifle. She scanned the living room. "Come out you little monster so that I can flatten your little germ-infested body," she wheezed between her clenched false teeth.

She took two hops toward the sofa when the mouse ran out from under it and momentarily froze under the glass-top coffee table.

In one swift, but clumsy movement, Dora grasped the broom handle with both hands and swung it around, knocking a lamp from a stand by the sofa and sending it crashing onto the floor, and bringing the broom down on the coffee table. The glass splintered, sending a small shard into Dora's right eye. Still holding the broom, she let out a loud yelp of pain and covered her injured eye with her hand.

The mouse ran past her, heading for the furnace vent at the base of a wall.

"Oh no you don't," Dora yelled. She raised the broom, swiveled about, and brought the bristles down hard on top of the mouse. Then she lost her balance and fell face-down on the floor. Her forehead smacked the hardwood floor so hard she was momentarily dazed. Through the blurred vision in her uninjured eye she watched the mouse crawl out from under the bristles, run to the vent, crawl through a hole, and out of sight.

"Nooooooo," Dora screamed. She smacked the floor with the palm of her hand.

She then felt a pain in her left arm that radiated to her chest. Then her heart stopped.

A week later when Dora was found, Albert was sitting next to her. A dead mouse dangled from his mouth.

The Tuesday Train

Peter Michal

The train stopped and two guys, one bearded and one clean-shaven, stepped on. They were young and broad-shouldered — the built to last types — and serious-looking. They walked to the back of the car and I put my head down and resumed my reading.

I looked up when one of the guys, the bearded one, walked past again. He walked to the front of the car and sat in the rear-facing seat by the door. The guy's eyes scanned the car, up and down the two columns of droopy heads.

The guy stood up and started back down the aisle. Before he came close and I lowered my eyes I saw it, the wire poking out of his unzipped bomber jacket.

The train pulled up at the next station. The two guys stepped off. That was the Monday train.

*

The Tuesday train came down the hill fast, slicing through the dense morning fog like a knife cutting the curd. The Girl and I stepped on at the bottom of the hill. We found our spot and I put my head down and tried to block out the drone of the diesel engine and read my book.

The train came to a long, shuddering halt. I looked up just as the doors opened and the two guys from the day before, wearing the same heavy clothes, got on.

This time there was a third guy, a fat man, and he sat down next to the ticket machine. The bearded one stood in the doorway and played with his phone while the clean-shaven one sat with a blank expression on his face, staring out the window into the misty nothingness on the other side.

The fat man stood up. He staggered to the doors and whispered into the lowered ear of the bearded one. The fat man pointed at someone at the front of the car and the bearded one, looking over, nodded his head. The fat man staggered back to his seat.

The bearded one took out yesterday's copy of the daily rag from his leather satchel and started up the aisle. The clean-shaven one followed his partner with his eyes. His face remained blank, a practiced expressionlessness which made him look not dumb but menacing.

I leaned forward and peered down the aisle. The bearded one was now sitting in the rear-facing seat at the front of the car. The top of his head bobbed over the folded-out newspaper.

I glanced back at the clean-shaven one. He kept looking over at his partner, the same blank expression on his face, but now he started rubbing the bulge in the right pocket of his overcoat.

I turned back to the bearded one. His head kept bobbing over the tabloid sheet.

The clean-shaven one kept rubbing the bulge in his overcoat like it was a hard-on.

I put my head down and pretended to read.

*

The train decelerated as it approached the last station before Central. I sensed a change in the situation, not from the expression on the clean-shaven one's face, which remained impassive and unrevealing, but from his right hand, which betrayed him as it recommenced rubbing the gun in the pocket of his overcoat.

I peered down the aisle to the front of the car just as a guy in a black leather cap and motorcycle jacket stood up. The bearded one, seated directly opposite, calmly lowered the newspaper.

I knew him! The tough-looking rider in the cap, I knew him!

I'd seen him on the train before. I'd once overheard him talking to a friend about his ex and how she'd robbed him blind and left him with nothing. The way he described it, you didn't want to be in the ex's shoes the next time he ran into her.

A second time I'd overheard the guy say he was getting his motorcycle permit back. Then he'd joked to his friend, 'It's only been seven years, hey!' Later I'd thought about that, what you had to do to get your license suspended for seven whole years? Kill someone on the road?

He was a real charmer.

He now walked up to the doors as the train inched its way along the platform to its mark. The bearded one stood up.

I glanced back at the clean-shaven one. He remained in his seat, eyes narrowed, staring like a hawk.

The train finally came to a stop. The doors sounded and then jerked open. The guy in the cap stepped out. The bearded one followed.

I turned back to the clean-shaven one but he was gone. The doors behind us chimed as they began closing. The fat man remained in his seat.

I turned my body and put my face flat against the glass and shielded my eyes from the light behind. I couldn't see them. Where the hell were they?

The train started pulling away slowly. I saw them now! We passed them on the platform. The bearded one was just behind the guy in the leather cap, the clean-shaven one trailing five steps back.

I stayed with them. Then I saw it. I saw it. I saw the bearded one come from behind and take down the guy in the cap. The clean-shaven one jumped on top, arms flaying, hitting.

He was still beating down on the guy when I lost them in the gloom.

I sat back down. The Girl and I looked at each other. I raised my eyebrows and she shrugged her shoulders.

*

The train came to its final stop. The doors opened. The fat man got out.

We got out last and slowly made our way through the station and out onto the street. It was drizzling and cold and I put the collar of my jacket up. Then we walked to our offices to start another day's work.

Victoria's Bath

Larry Lefkowitz

Since he began working on the unfinished book of Lieberman, her late husband, he had "carte blanche" (in Victoria's words) to her apartment, subject to the condition that he always telephone prior to coming. She turned down his suggestion that she give him a duplicate key. This arrangement allowed him to work on the book in her apartment as well as to facilitate his romantic pursuit of Victoria. Her limitations on his free access invariably raised his suspicions of possible Victorian liaisons with other suitors.

Victoria, in her bath, heard Kunzman open the door to her apartment. A musician, she was blessed with good ears. "In here," Kunzman heard Victoria call him from the bathroom. He thought of Actaeon who, according to the charming Greek myth, surprised the goddess Diana while she was bathing naked and who was turned into a stag in punishment and torn to pieces by his own dogs. Tiresias fared slightly better than Actaeon: he was blinded by Athena after he stumbled onto her bathing naked. (And they say the Jews have an angry God.)

Entering the bathroom, he found his naiad in her bubbled bath, naked as Venus emerging from the foamy waves in Bottecelli's painting. Victoria was lying, her upper body above the water, her arms crossed in front of her chest in the style of Egyptian pharaohs depicted in temple paintings. Victoria constituted, without doubt, an adornment to the bath.

Kunzman stared at her blankly. She raised her hands and shook them like a belly dancer (or maybe Salome in her famous dance). "Queen of the Bathtub," she announced in good spirits.

He didn't know what was expected of him.

She told him. "Come join me," she said in a voluptuous whisper, extending her arms toward him in invitation. She wore her cat-that-stole-the-cream smile. Her eyes bore into him with Kama Sutra seductiveness.

"Get undressed?" he inquired of her.

She lowered her arms in exasperation (he strove not to stare at her breasts). "People usually do before they enter the bath."

It dawned on him that she wasn't interested in his cleanliness.

"It's not my style," he informed her. It wasn't.

She glowered at him. "You and Nitza never ... ?"

Nu, and her and Lieberman in the bathtub. Kunzman shut his mind to the thought.

Her invasion of his privacy rankled. Kunzman said nothing. His saying nothing in turn rankled her. "Maybe you prefer a waterbed?" she taunted.

Kunzman decided retreat was the prudent course given Victoria's mood. He would go work on the book. As he left the bathroom, pursued by his inamorata's heaped honorifics: *"zeide, schlemiel, schlimazel"* followed by *"Ikh hob dikh in bod"* (To hell with you) − once again, the diva-dame in one of her *groyser kundes* (big stick) moods; Diotoma, Socrates' love-instructress, had become Xanthippe, Socrates' shrewish wife, Yiddish curses having replaced Greek ones. He feared being struck by an object from her Venetian glass collection, perhaps the kitsch (in his eyes) dolphin which lay on a glass shelf in arm's reach of the bathtub. Why, Kunzman reflected, couldn't I have a mistress like that of Herzog in Bellow's (eponymous) novel who is kind and beautiful and has a religion of sex which she believes can cure Herzog's ailments? Yet he knew by now that such a mistress's cure, however kind and well-intended, might only add to his own ailments.

He retreated from the wrath of the caladarium to the inner sanctum of the scriptorium, having considered but immediately rejected taking a parting shot at Victoria, like the Parthians who fired arrows over their shoulder while retreating from battle. He recalled that Victoria said to him once, "You always seem as if you are looking for an escape route." This remark had struck him as uncharacteristically astute. It, or his present predicament, conjured up before his eyes Cigoli's painting 'Joseph and Potiphar's Wife' together with the biblical inspiration for it: 'And she caught him by his robe saying, "lie with me" and he left his garment in her hand, and fled.' He wondered if his passivity was not a goad to Victoria. As the poet Zelda put it:

When I see how complacent you are
Something inside me runs wild.

Safely in his work-room, he began turning over one by one the items of Lieberman's corpus, so insulted and incensed that he paid no attention to what was written on them. The imagined picture of Victoria and Lieberman naked in the bath pursued him.

After some minutes Victoria's voice, softer, called him. The softness decided him despite his knowledge that when Victoria was being overly sweet a threat hung in the air; Kunzman had always been a patsy for softness, for *heindelach*. He put aside his being miffed, his being the *klutz*, his *hors de combat* status and, returning to the bathroom, entered.

She was still in the bathtub, looking like nothing so much as a pouting seal whose ball had fallen from its nose during a performance. "Come on, Kunzman, let go of your poor-little-boy mood. I only wanted to surprise you," she purred honey-voiced. "Give me a hug."

Kunzman redux. He complied, despite thoroughly soaking his shirt and pants in the process; as he did so, he wondered if he wasn't but a trampist on the consciousness of others.

Crucible

Joseph Allison

A forest of ancient oak grew outside the walls of Elderwood. During harvest time music would play and ale would flow but now there was only an ashy shadow on the land where the town once stood.

Mary lowered her spyglass, loaded a bolt into her crossbow and heaved back the string. She'd found her way home.

Her crossbow was resting loosely in her hands by the time she walked through the remains of the old portcullis. The town hall was the only recognisable shape, that and the church where she'd got married. A keystone lay scattered beside the path, still engraved with the town's coat of arms, a white tree on a navy background.

She'd expected more to be left behind. Everything had burned in the dragon's flame. Log cabins became charcoal. Bodies became bonemeal. Swords and shovels all returned to shining lumps in black dirt. Everything Elderwood ever was crunched beneath her boots. Everyone she'd ever known had lived in that town. Some she would never know. As she reached what had been the fire's epicentre, her body began to shake as her mind burned with rage.

The dragon had attacked in autumn. She'd gone hunting, deep in the forest when suddenly, she'd felt a change in the wind. It faded then came again. All the birds fell silent, as a roar of anger shook the ground. The dragon passed over her, making the forest tremble with each beat of its wings.

She remembered running, the fire, the destruction, the heat, the screams. She remembered her own screams. Often, she tried not to.

A black mountain stood above the town like a shadow reaching into the sky. She let her mind cool but her memories kept their shape. Now, the hunt began. She kept her eyes forward as, towards the indifferent mountain, she trudged.

She'd tracked the dragon to a cave on the western side of the mountain. The air was warmed by geysers that erupted acrid steam. She placed a gas-mask over her face. The air was poisonous to humans but, perhaps, it didn't affect larger beasts. A dragon could hide there.

A hiss escaped the cave. She froze. She gazed into the deep tunnel, then made her way down into the darkness ahead.

She came to an underground cavern illuminated by glowing stones. There were bones. Most were animals. Some were soldiers wearing the armour of the Elderwood guard and at the centre were the gigantic bones of a dragon. A sword had split the top of its skull. A jet of steam hissed from a crack in the floor.

She approached the dragon's remains and reached for its snout. Her fingers curled into a fist and beat the side of the bone with all her rage.

Suddenly she froze, as she realised nothing made sense.

A scaly serpentine neck lifted itself from the darkness followed closely by the head of a white she-dragon.

Mary stood, petrified.

The dragon flicked its eyes open. Its eyeballs were silver and featureless like two drops of mercury resting on the surface of its scales, the colour of ash. It curled its body around the remains of the fallen dragon and placed the tip of its snout in front of her. Pain weighed heavily on the dragon's brow. Its chest wheezed in the poisonous air. It considered Mary with interest. Suddenly an alien thought engulfed Mary's mind:

A white tree on a navy background.

The thought came from a mind similar to hers but the anger and fear that moved in its wake were ancient and deep. They were a dragon's thoughts.

"Elderwood…scares you?"

Images came wordlessly:

The Elderwood banner.

Two dragons, one black, one white.

Sword.

Crossbow.

Question.

"I'm-! …What?"

Her crossbow.

Question.

Mary wondered how many bolts it would've taken to kill the dragon. She realised she already knew the crossbow would've been useless. She had come to fight a monster and die. She knew now, the dragon *couldn't* fight. Its skin crumbled as it struggled for breath, like ash on dying embers.

She lowered her crossbow and dropped it.

"Tell me what happened."

Memories played in her head and, gradually, Mary began to understand.

For centuries, the two dragons' love grew beneath the mountain.

Dragons feasted rarely and travelled regularly but they found the hunting grounds plentiful, so settled without much thought to the town flourishing nearby.

One day, the dragon went hunting while her mate was asleep and returned to find blood, everywhere.

An anger raged through her soul, cracking the mountain and releasing poison into the air.

"And so you killed them and the people who sent them, and everyone who knew their names... and hid here until the air began to poison you."

The dragon's thoughts inclined to the word: **Yes.**

"Why didn't you kill me and complete your revenge? More to the point, why don't you leave this place if you know it's hurting you?"

The dragon allowed her question to echo back: **Why don't you leave this place if you know it's hurting you?**

It probed Mary's memories. She saw every night she spent counting the dead, every fiery nightmare, every day she'd spent planning her revenge.

Mary shook her head.

"Listen, I know I'm one of the few people who could understand, but there's no forgiveness here."

No.

"Did killing them help?"

No.

"Did it even make you happy?"

No.

"You had power, you won…*everyone* died…you sacrificed all those lives to your wrath and…nothing."

Yes.

"Then it was pointless."

Yes.

"That's *almost* the worst thing about this. Remember that. *Promise.*"

I promise.

She picked up her crossbow and looked at herself in the dragon's eyes.

"You'll die here. If that's your choice…I hope you die…soon."

The dragon closed its eyes, in thanks, and slumbered.

Mary left Elderwood behind her. An oak forest still grows outside Elderwood and someday, from black dirt, new life would grow.

The Recent History of the Sánchez Family Tragedies: Part V

Guilie Castillo Oriard

Motive is a finicky thing. Causality and correlation can be deceptive, unless you have the whole story. In all stories, but especially in the history of a family like ours, it really is all about context. Facts are the least interesting ingredient.

Yes, your grandfather did kill his brother. The question you should be asking, though, isn't *what* happened but *why*, and—maybe most importantly—how it came to happen at all.

History is full of murderous siblings; I've no idea why the concept of *brotherly love* still survives. We trust these other children of our parents, we treat them as a part of ourselves, and we abide by this forced kinship as if blood ties guaranteed not just love but empathy. All too often these people turn out to be as separate from us, as alien, as if they'd been born on the other side of the world. Worse, because they come with grudges. And they know altogether too much about us.

The seeds were there from the beginning. Even before Toño, or even your grandfather, Anselmo, were born. Seeds of iniquity, of wrongs wrought in the name of the best intentions.

That this all ended in tragedy surprised no one; that it didn't happen sooner did.

And, also, that it was Toño who died.

Anselmo was always the loose cannon. Quick-tempered, flying into epic rages over nothing. Today he'd be diagnosed with attention deficit disorder, maybe on the autistic spectrum. Back then, he was just a problem child. He figured out himself ways to cope, much as he learned, in order to avoid the schoolmaster's cane, to use the right hand instead of his natural left.

My mother remembers those rages happening all the time when she was growing up. Maybe a child's tendency to exaggerate; she would've been only four when Anselmo was twelve, the year Toño was born. The year when Anselmo went rogue. He had been 'difficult' before, but in adolescence he became positively mutinous. Overnight, it seemed, he ceased to fear The Doctor, his stepfather, and no escalation in whippings or punishment appeared to have any effect other than to make him more defiant. He ran away several times, disappearing for days; around the time he was fifteen he was gone for over a month. He'd been staying with a much older, and divorced, woman. She kicked him out after he punched a hole in her wall during an argument over some chipped chinaware.

He joined a gang, got into fights (with knives, someone once let slip), but he was never violent with anyone in the family. Except The Doctor, just that once when he came home to his mother with a swollen jaw and a bloody nose—nothing new, but this time he did something about it. Curiously, though, there was no 'rage' then; only two punches, the second of which landed The Doctor flat on the ground.

Toño never forgave Anselmo for it. *Dunno why you didn't do it years before*, he'd say, only half joking. And Anselmo, in his characteristic tactless honesty, would cut to the marrow of the issue: *You're just jealous because you never dared to do it yourself.*

Toño despised Anselmo. Toño was the quiet type, with big, guileless, dark green eyes that seemed to swallow you whole, and a sensitive, rather feminine mouth that rarely smiled, rarely spoke harshly or loudly. I never heard Toño use a vulgar word (Anselmo could make a sailor blush). Toño lived by a strict code of discipline, integrity, and modesty—and he judged everyone by those same standards: if he could do it, why couldn't everyone else? Anselmo fell short by light-years. See him through Toño's eyes: loud, unruly, unpredictable, perhaps even dangerous (Anselmo was a consummate practical joker and Toño—the youngest, the most serious and thus the most fun to pick on—became the preferred target for every prank). Anselmo must have seemed arrogant, irresponsible, expansive and overbearing—everything, in short, that Toño reviled.

And yet, he seemed to follow in his brother's steps. Anselmo did a year of medical school (dropped out when he realized, a tad late, he couldn't stand the sight of blood); twelve years later, Toño did three (and then dropped out, too). Anselmo graduated *summa cum laude* from the country's most prestigious architecture program; Toño applied to the same school and even repeated a course in order to graduate with an average two hundredths higher than Anselmo. He sought internships where his brother had done his, he drove similar cars, dated similar types in women. Was it admiration, a sort of tribute? Was it competition? Even, maybe, in some warped, dysfunctional way, an attempt to diminish whatever his brother did? *I can do it, too. See? Nothing special about it. Or about you.*

It's always the quiet ones. Anselmo's rages may have been fearsome, but they were flare, not blaze. His anger burned fast, and once it was gone, *it was gone.* But Toño never let his anger out. He held on to every wrong, every slight, every moment of inadequacy, and balled it up tight in an intimate crook of his psyche. And he kept the fire at a constant, slow burn. As the years passed, every impurity was consumed, and left behind only the purest, unadulterated wrath.

And wrath magnifies everything.

So, yes, when I got the call about a murder in *Villa del Bosque* I had every reason to assume Anselmo was the victim. In the confusion, I gave the police Toño's description as the probable murderer, and that's how the first warrant went out. In those first days, when the murderer might still have been on the move and perhaps more easily spotted at a bus station or the highway checkpoints, the police were looking for the wrong man. Because of me. By the time they figured out that the description matched not a man on the run but a body at the morgue, it was too late.

Without Compass

Cynthia Leslie-Bole

She can see that damn fool leaning forward, gesticulating to Carl as though what he has to say is actually interesting. She hates the sparseness of the hair on his head, the mousy gray color it has turned over the years. The thickness of his fingers seems calculated to annoy her, and the grease that never comes clean from under his nails makes her cringe when he gestures. And look at Carl, trusty side-kick, gullible mascot who thinks Eddie can do no wrong. Eddie could tell Carl to eat dog shit and he'd actually do it. The wipers smear droplets around in the grime that has accreted on the windshield. Yet another thing Eddie is supposed to take care of but doesn't: washing the car.

Verna arrived home tonight with her feet killing her after her shift at Safeway got out, only to find an empty house, no dinner on the table, and no Eddie anywhere. The deal was that she made breakfast and he made dinner. So where was that lazy slob? She called out "Eddie!" and her voice just echoed around her. The rest of the house was stone cold and dark. Then Verna noticed a piece of paper on the table and felt her heart jump.

"Is this what I think it is?" she wondered. "It figures if it is. Such a cliché. Everything Eddie has ever done has been done a thousand times before."

She knew what the note would say, but she read it anyway,

scoffing at his misspelling of the word harpy and his utter inability to use punctuation. "Idiot," she thought. "I never shoulda married a guy without an education." But then Verna surprised herself by choking up. "Well old gal, I guess this is what you've been wanting for a long time, so why aren't you happy about it?"

Verna sat down at the kitchen table, uncharacteristically at a loss for how to proceed. She didn't know if she should make some dinner, call her mother, or just keep sitting there to see if anything else would happen. She gave the latter a try for about five minutes, then let out a snort of disgust at herself.

"Get your butt outa this chair, girl," she chided herself. "Don't let that asshole get the last word. You gotta come out on top of this thing, let him know who's boss."

Verna grabbed her purse, buttoned her coat, and headed out the door. She knew where to look; Eddie only ever went three places: The Shamrock Pub, Carl's house, or the Owl's Nest diner. Given the time, she had a hunch his stomach would lead him to the diner, so she decided to try there first.

But now that she's sitting here, hands on the steering wheel and watching his sorry old self through the window, Verna doesn't know what to do. Eddie has decided to leave her. He has actually decided to do something without her prodding for the first time since the accident.

It wasn't supposed to be this way. She had fantasized for years that she would be the one to break the deadening logjam that had piled up between them after they lost Eddie Jr. twelve years ago. She was going to leave him with a great show of jaunty independence. She was going to make something new for herself and leave him crying in the dust, just as he deserved after all those years of stony silence and sleeping in the sewing room. She was gonna show him she could still turn heads and get a little action going for herself. But she never quite got around to it. And now the bastard had beat her to the punch.

"Didn't know he had it in him," she thinks, still clutching the steering wheel to keep her tethered to the known universe.

Verna sees Eddie lean forward, and she unconsciously echoes his movement in the car. She squints through the smudges to see better. She sees Eddie wipe his face and Carl reach out a hand toward him. She decides he's having a coughing fit, maybe choking—that would serve him right. But then she notices his shoulders shaking and face contorting.

It takes a moment for what she is seeing to sink in. Eddie is crying. The bastard is actually crying! And sycophantic Carl is trying to comfort him. Verna doesn't know what to think. She has never seen Eddie cry in the 39 years they'd been married, not even when their only child was killed in a car wreck. Why didn't he cry with her when she needed some company in her grief?

And now what is she supposed to do? She can't very well storm in there and give him a piece of her mind when he's sobbing like a baby, can she? What does it mean? Why is he crying, in the diner of all places? Now, of all times? Does he still love her? Is he actually pained by what he's doing? The thought twists something small and frozen in Verna's chest.

"What the hell!" she mutters out loud, "fuck him and his too-late tears." Then she pops the car in gear and speeds out into the rainy night, with no idea at all which direction she should go.

H-O-M-E

Alex Reece Abbott

Jim is jammed in the corner of the retro-chic cafe, buffing rain-drops off the *Jaguar* fob on his keyring and pondering how women decorated before Cath Kidston.

"Isn't that right, Jim?" says Jane.

"Absolutely." Jim stops counting forget-me-nots on the pink vinyl tablecloth and orders another coffee.

"*Americano* alright?" says the waitress.

"Don't mind where it's from, long as it's hot and strong," he says.

Brenda nudges him. "Oh Jim, you are a one."

"Isn't he." Jane rolls her eyes at her sister. "Mizzling again. Why didn't you remind me to bring my new umbrella, Jim?"

"Very quiet today, James," says Brenda. "Have we Christmas-shopped you out? Got a lot on with getting ready for the bungalow..."

He smiles at her.

"I'm cream-crackered, I'll tell you that for nowt," says Jane. "Spent all last week going through the attic like a dose of salts, didn't I?"

Jim gulps a mouthful of coffee and pats his scalded lips with a rosebud napkin. "She did."

"We're moving and my husband – Lord of the Manor here – goes off playing golf," says Jane, as though no woman has been more widowed by the royal and ancient game.

Jim folds his arms. "County seniors championship."

"How did you get on?" says Brenda.

"Got rid of loads of stuff," says Jane, before he can answer. "The *Ladybirds* went years ago. I picked out our Sam's favourite books for his kids...I'm not even sure they read — "

"— Dyslexic? There's a lot of that nowadays. They don't do books. Prefer their *PlayStations*." Brenda clicks her tongue. "Not like our day."

Jane stirs her Darjeeling. "I found a cardboard suitcase hidden away, stuffed full of *Matchbox* cars, some still in their boxes."

"Worth a fortune with original packaging, so *Antiques Roadshow* say," says Brenda, leaning forward. "Can't put a price on memories though."

Jim grips his keys, a tip cutting into his palm. The café is brimming with distressed pine and nostalgia – a retro-style duck-egg green cake-mixer, floral plates and stacked decoupaged boxes. On a battered bookcase, surrounded by knick-knacks, four large, wooden letters – suitably chipped and bruised – spell H-O-M-E.

Jane leans forward. "The *Rolls Royce* and *E-Type Jag* were good as new...perfect stocking fillers for the girls. I gave all the others to Oxfam. No point leaving them lying around going to waste."

"Parking." Jim lurches into the street, leaving a wake of scattered sugar-cubes.

Jane rests her vintage bone china teacup on its mismatched saucer and smiles at Brenda. "Sometimes you have to be brutal."

Brenda places a saucer over Jim's coffee to keep it warm. "Look, it's siling down now."

Topping up the parking meter, Jim sees Jane's *Lulu Guinness* brolly on the backseat of their *Skoda* station wagon. On the way back to the café, he takes a snickleway and hurls the umbrella into a builder's skip.

Jane moves aside and he squeezes into his seat.

"You're drenched," says Brenda. "No ticket – did you win?"

Jim smiles and swills the last of his coffee. "All sorted."

How do you solve a problem like the patriarchy: A plaintive reflection on character arcs in *The Sound of Music*

Flora Gaugg

We need to talk about Maria: the golden-haired free spirit who can be found twirling atop mountains, singing gaily all the while. At the film's outset our heroine in hand-me-downs is a rebel nun. She flouts the rules of the tutting nuns with her uncouth running and singing in the Abbey. She is 'always late for everything, except for every meal' (frolicking over the Austrian hillside tends to make one peckish). Maria's joyous spirit cannot be stifled, even by the pious old nuns who consider her a problem that needs solving.

In a pleasing departure from the standard model, Maria's search for meaning is not in marriage, nor in the acceptance of a man. Instead she seeks personal fulfilment and, ultimately, to do some good in the world. Even when her spiritual search is thrown off course, she accepts the challenge of playing governess to seven strange (in every sense of the word) children with alacrity, proclaiming her confidence in exuberant, suitcase-swinging song.

Her defiance is dismissed as insolence by the dauntingly handsome Captain von Trapp, when she refuses to answer to his whistle:

> **Maria**: Oh, no, sir. I'm sorry, sir. I could never answer to a whistle. Whistles are for dogs and cats and other animals, but not for children and definitely not for me. It would be too... humiliating.
>
> **Captain von Trapp:** Fräulein, were you this much trouble at the Abbey?
>
> **Maria:** Oh, much more, sir.

Of course, the children are awful. The seven little twerps use every prank in their arsenal in an attempt to rattle Maria and send her back to the Abbey a quivering mess. Yet Maria, surely valuing her vow of celibacy at this stage, refuses defeat. With little more than some gently sarcastic words over dinner, she manages to reduce all seven children to tears of shame.

Maria proves herself to be somewhat of a renaissance woman. She is an accomplished guitarist who can fashion play clothes from old drapes and teach seven tone-deaf children to sing in perfect harmony while juggling oranges. Maria brings some sorely needed joy to an otherwise bleak and miserable home.

Sadly and predictably, *The Sound of Music* (Wise, 1965) is not without its problematic depictions of women. Firstly there is the worrying admonishment of Nazi traitor scum, Rolph, that sixteen year old Liesl 'need[s] someone older and wiser telling [her] what to do', and the insane implication that he, being a whole year older, is qualified to be that someone.

There is also the demonisation of Baroness Schraeder whose central character flaw seems to be her inability to relate to seven weird children who, as we've already established, are frightful. The glamorous Baroness is bizarrely cast as a villain based solely on her lack of maternal talent, which the film seems to suggest somehow renders her undeserving of Captain von Trapp's affection.

Amongst such troubling examples, Maria stands out as a beacon of hope. Then, she gets married.

Maria manages to disarm the Captain with her guileless charm, and in one of the least joyous and most funeral-like weddings ever portrayed on film, they tie the knot.

Don't get me wrong, post-marriage Maria is still a force with which to be reckoned. She outsmarts Nazis and hoofs it over the border to Switzerland. However, the moment she becomes Mrs von Trapp, the reckless energy that once defined her seems to evaporate. She trades in her home-spun clothing for sensible, feminine frocks. Her rough-and-tumble attitude is replaced with demure composure. She suddenly loses the goofy relationship she once had with the kids, and becomes a model mother seemingly overnight. She adopts an ethereal poise that is a far cry from the clumsy, flawed (read: human) woman she was before she said 'I do'.

Where's the sass? The chutzpah? With each viewing of the film I feel that familiar third act frustration as I see Maria tamed into a background-dwelling door mat.

How do you solve a problem like Maria? Instead I ask: Why is a disobedient female considered problematic?

The Way People Do When They're Falling Asleep

Nod Ghosh

Marcus Heaton. I force myself to say his name, though it tastes of disaster. I close my eyes, and I'm there again. I don't know how to deal with the feelings that follow.

His breathing is ragged and uneven. He twitches the way people do when they're falling asleep.

When we arrived at the beach hut, he'd lingered outside the bathroom while I took a piss. Maybe he was standing guard so I didn't do a runner, though I couldn't have escaped through that icy slit of a window. Maybe the sound of my peeing aroused him. Dirty bastard. I despised Marcus, yet being in the hands of this deranged being was all I deserved.

I had let him do what he wanted. And I'd let him do it again.

*

On the third night, we drank homebrewed wine. The blue-red fluid had undertones of guava and raw sewage. We drank more. He didn't see me slip four of his sleeping pills into the enamel cup. I sipped my wine, crouched on the floor and stroked his leg. It wasn't easy. I was huge back then.

I stooped between his legs, smelled his mushroom gusset. Something creaked. I opened his fly. His erection sprang through the 'Y' of his underpants and I took him between my lips. The dank taste of man reached my throat and threatened to gag me.

He clasped my hair in his fist. I sank my nails into the turkey skin behind his knee, allowed my incisors to graze the bulb of his penis. He shuddered as I forced him under my control. This man. This ugly little man, with his hesitancy, his shiny scalp and his peculiar brown clothes. This man who had taken me as his plaything.

Well, I was going to be the one who made the decisions. I *was* going to be the one in charge. Not him.

My jaw increased the intensity of its work, like chewing on gum. He whimpered like a schoolgirl.

"Don't stop," he sighed.

So I released the suction, squeezed his scrotum and pulled away. He made a sound, a high-pitched appeal.

In the corner of the hut, the shelves were piled with tools and hunting gear. I took a knife from its leather sheath and pulled the end from a roll of duct tape. The tape was grey, the same grey as his eyes. He watched me. I cut a piece of tape with the knife.

He watched as if measuring my every move. His trousers were wrapped around his ankles and he nearly fell when I led him to the bed. I laid him down and strapped his legs together with tape. He never flinched, never asked what I was doing.

So I carried on.

Arms to the bedstead. He sighed in private ecstasy.

I taped over his mouth.

That was when I detected the first hint of uncertainty. He was still aroused though, his cock pointing to his chin like an arrow. His nipples contracted when I unbuttoned his shirt. I traced the contours of his skin with my finger. The bed slumped under my weight, and the air rushed out of his lungs when I straddled him. I manoeuvred his member towards the valley between my legs. But instead of taking him, I pulled away.

He groaned from behind his gag. His eyes beseeched me, begging me to carry on.

I positioned the knife over his sternum. His muffled moans ceased and his dick deflated. The tip of the blade penetrated his chest.

You can tell when someone is screaming, even through duct tape.

"Don't worry," I said.

Now it was my turn to have fun.

I carved a circle the size of a dinner plate, careful not to penetrate the skin deeply. More screams. Tears ran down the side of his face. He lunged and the knife slipped in a little further. It made a wet sound when I pulled it out. His tone changed. He was crying, big heaving sobs, through the tape.

I carried on. The cries became insistent, but I didn't let them distract me. The gaps between his screams increased. He stopped thrashing, like he'd learned it would hurt less if he kept still, or maybe because he couldn't move anymore. My hand wasn't as steady as it might have been. Must have been the homebrew. My knee sat in a pool of blood.

I made a smaller circle inside the larger one. Then I cut the segments.

I drew an iris.

I drew part of an eye on his chest.

When I finished, he'd stopped moving. The bed was swimming in crimson. His wounds were coagulating. They formed broad ribbons on his chest. His mouth seemed to have clotted shut too. His eyes were focussed on a point behind my head. Glassy grey.

I went to the bathroom and washed myself, splashed in tepid water and rinsed all traces of him from my body.

The log burner glowed red, like a dying star.

His breathing is ragged and uneven.

He thought he could take me, like I was nothing. Thought he could slip into my body in the middle of the night, pulling my flesh like he was kneading dough.

He didn't anticipate what was coming. He didn't know I'd be the one who fucked him over, not the other way round.

Marcus lay in a pool of blood. I pulled the blanket over his face, so I didn't have to see him.

His name tastes of disaster, but in the end, it all comes from me. I am the devil in all of this.

His breathing is ragged and uneven. He twitches the way people do when they're falling asleep.

I took a roll of bank notes from his wallet, found his keys and unlocked the door. I walked into the grey air, didn't look back.

Also from Pure Slush Books

https://pureslush.com/store/

- Sloth 7 Deadly Sins Vol. 4
ISBN: 978-1-925536-66-9 (paperback) / 978-1-925536-67-6 (eBook)
- Greed 7 Deadly Sins Vol. 3
ISBN: 978-1-925536-64-5 (paperback) / 978-1-925536-65-2 (eBook)
- Gluttony 7 Deadly Sins Vol. 2
ISBN: 978-1-925536-54-6 (paperback) / 978-1-925536-55-3 (eBook)
- Lust 7 Deadly Sins Vol. 1
ISBN: 978-1-925536-47-8 (paperback) / 978-1-925536-48-5 (eBook)
- Happy² Pure Slush Vol. 15
ISBN: 978-1-925536-39-3 (paperback) / 978-1-925536-40-9 (eBook)
- Inane Pure Slush Vol. 14
ISBN: 978-1-925536-17-1 (paperback) / 978-1-925536-18-8 (eBook)